BLAZE!

BITTER VALLEY

Wayne D. Dundee

Blaze! Bitter Valley by Wayne D. Dundee
Text Copyright 2015 by Wayne D. Dundee
Series Concept and Characters Copyright 2015 by Stephen
Mertz
Cover Design by Livia Reasoner
The Book Place

All rights reserved.

ISBN-13: 978-0692359020 (Rough Edges Press)
ISBN-10: 0692359028

Blaze Western Series

Chapter 1

For the first time since they had met, married, and then stayed in business together as gunfighters, Kate and J.D. Blaze were taking a brief vacation.

"The honeymoon we never had," Kate called it.

Sunshine filtered through a gentle breeze. Their horses were staked a short distance away in a stand of lush grass on a secluded slope that overlooked a stream. The kitchen staff at the Lodge had prepared a picnic lunch of fried chicken, boiled corn on the cob, fresh biscuits, thick wedges of apple pie, and a bottle of highly regarded house wine. Nearby, water spilled from a rocky ledge to become a glittering waterfall.

Everything was perfect.

That is, until J.D., distracted by something, abruptly interrupted a lingering kiss.

Beside him on the blanket, Kate blinked.

"What's the matter, hon?"

J.D. frowned. "Didn't you hear that?...Can't you feel it in the ground?"

"What are you talking about?"

"There it is again. Can't you feel that?"

Suddenly Kate's eyes widened as she *did* begin to sense it, too. The ground beneath their picnic blanket seemed to be shivering faintly.

The shivering intensified, accompanied by a low rumble that gradually grew louder and louder. And then high-pitched yips, unmistakably of human origin, entered the mix.

"There!" said Kate, pointing past J.D.'s shoulder, her arm slanted at an upward angle.

J.D.'s face snapped around, following the line of her finger. At the crest of the slope, a hundred yards up from the spot they'd selected for their picnic spread, he saw the source of what was sending tremors through the ground.

A well-appointed buggy drawn by a team of sleek black horses was racing along the crest at breakneck speed. The man and woman on the cushioned seat of the buggy were clinging partly to one another and partly to grips on either end of the seat. No sign of reins to control the team extended back to the driver's box—the conveyance was a runaway!

Galloping only a short distance behind the buggy, three riders were spurring their horses to keep pace. Two of them had their hats off, whirling them wildly above their heads as they occasionally emitted loud whoops. A third, as Kate and J.D. watched, drew a pistol from the holster on his hip and fired two rounds into the air.

Through clenched teeth, Kate said, "That doesn't look good."

"Especially not for those poor damn fools in the buggy," J.D. agreed. "They've either dropped or had their reins cut. That's a runaway rig!"

"And those riders coming up behind aren't giving chase to try and help, are they?"

"Not by a damn sight. I'd even go so far as to guess they might somehow be responsible for the loss of those reins and for spooking that team to begin with."

As they talked, the pair had risen to their feet and hurriedly began re-arranging themselves. They moved swiftly, with no wasted motions. Simultaneously, they leaned over to seize the gun belts they had discarded earlier to more comfortably stretch out for the meal and what had been about to follow.

J.D. paused momentarily to drink in the sight of his stunning wife as she stood there, still with a bit of a flush coloring her high cheekbones, adjusting the holstered .44-40 Colt riding just above the luscious swell of her hips. Above the hips, a narrow waist flowed up into a set of strong, wide shoulders balancing a pair of high, firm breasts that strained the material of her blouse. Surrounding a flawlessly featured face accentuated by sparkling wide-set green eyes was a swirl of thick honey blonde hair frequently pulled back into a pony tail but today cascading free and loose.

J.D. could never help but marvel at how lovely she looked and how damn lucky he was to have her in his life.

Although it wasn't for him to say, of course, but the two of them made quite a striking pair. With his powerful physique, cougar-like grace, and a strong-jawed countenance highlighted by alert blue eyes that could burn hot with passion or turn dangerously ice cold, J.D. seldom failed to turn nearly as many female heads as Kate turned male ones. There was a time when his awareness of this had led him to cut quite a swath through the feminine population of the West, but since meeting Kate those days were past.

"You know, we can't be certain the couple in the buggy are purely innocent victims," Kate pointed out, jerking J.D. from his brief reverie. "They might have done something to deserve being chased the way they are."

J.D. shook his head. "Nobody deserves that kind of treatment, not to be trapped on a runaway rig in rugged country like this. Getting driven over a mountain cliff is a helluva nasty way to check out—to say nothing of the innocent horses who'll get dragged along in the bargain."

Once more moving in concert, they leaned to snatch up

the hats they'd also set aside earlier—a flat-crowned Stetson for Kate and also a Stetson, though one with a bit more sweep to the brim and height to the crown, for J.D.

Be-hatted and armed, they ran to the horses.

"How are we going to play this?" Kate asked as they sprang into their saddles then wheeled the animals and spurred toward the crest of the slope.

Chapter 2

The plan J.D. and Kate decided on was pretty basic. Since they were joining the party a little late, they would have to close on the hoorahing riders from behind. Hopefully, the sight of outside involvement would be enough to cause the three to veer away and give up their pursuit. But if they weren't smart enough to take a hint, then Kate would hang back and call upon her skills with a gun to provide however much added persuasion it took to get rid of them. While she was thus occupied, it fell for J.D. to focus on trying to catch up with the wildly fleeing buggy. The trick then would be for him to find some way to bring its panicked team of horses under control before it was too late.

When first spotted, the buggy and its pursuers were moving east to west—left to right in the Blazes' initial field of vision—across a flat, open expanse atop a long, broad hogback. By the time J.D. and Kate reached the top of the slope and turned to give chase, the buggy was out of sight and the riders were only murky slivers of shapes all but lost in the dust haze they were kicking up.

As J.D. and Kate urged their mounts to close the gap on the dust-blurred figures, the hogback began to narrow and twist downward at a moderate angle. The thick stands of evergreen, along with other types of trees and underbrush that had been flashing by on either side, started to thin and be replaced by more frequent outcroppings of rock. The carpeting of grass that had at first capped the hogback now gave way to patches of bared ground and gravel. Dust boiled up thicker under the horses' pounding hooves.

J.D. and Kate drew nearly even with the hindmost of the three horsemen, a tall, slender form astride a black and white pinto. Up to that point, they'd been running stirrup to stirrup with each other. At a faint signal from J.D., they spread wider apart and Kate took the lead, moving up alongside the unsuspecting rider on his right. When the man suddenly became aware of her presence, the grim expression on his pinched face turned into one of almost comical shock.

At that moment, J.D. came up unnoticed on the man's left. Leaning out and down from his saddle, while still racing along at full gallop, J.D. swept his muscular arm in a choppy backhand that knocked the distracted rider's foot out of its stirrup. As the foot instinctively sought to thrust itself back into place, J.D. clamped the rider's leg just above the ankle and jerked upward.

Caught off guard, still rattled by the appearance of Kate on the other side of him, the man was easily unbalanced. Emitting a frantic yelp, he toppled out of his saddle, hit the ground hard, and was left tumbling and rolling in the dusty wake of the still-running horses.

J.D. and Kate exchanged quick, rake-hell grins as they continued to race on after the remaining two horsemen.

But the element of surprise was lost now, the toppled rider's yelp having warned his comrades. When the faces of the two men up ahead turned to look back, they registered a fleeting moment of being startled. But when their eyes cut to the empty saddle of the third man, his horse only just beginning to break stride and slow down, their expressions hardened with anger and menace.

The rider who had fired the two shots still had his gun

drawn and clutched in one hand. After rein-whipping his horse to try and make it go faster, he twisted in his saddle and started to bring the gun around, clearly intending to fire back at those on his tail.

Kate's right hand swung down and then up again in a blur of speed and when it was extended at arm's length out in front of her, it was fisting a gleaming .44-40 Colt. Without hesitation and with accuracy born from hours of tireless practice, she took snap aim and fired. The shot cleanly blew the hat off the head of the would-be pistoleer and an instant later a second round passed so close to the tip of his nose that the heat from the sizzling slug singed the hair in his nostrils.

The warning shots were enough to convince the rider. He tried clumsily, frantically to re-holster his gun and lost it altogether, leaving it to clatter away on the rocks. He paid no further attention, concentrating instead on just facing forward. Seizing his reins in both hands, he then jerked his horse off-trail, abandoning the chase and fleeing off down through the rock-studded pines and underbrush of the south slope.

The gun hand of the remaining horseman froze with the pistol it had been reaching for only half-cleared of its holster. Suddenly finding himself on the wrong end of two-to-one odds, the man lost all will to continue putting up a running fight. Before any more shots could be fired, he shoved the pistol deep back into leather and sharp-reined his own horse off the opposite side of the hogback's crest, also abandoning the chase.

A short distance beyond where the two men had peeled off, Kate and J.D. slowed their horses briefly.

J.D. was grinning. "Hell, that was easy."

"Maybe too easy," Kate countered, not smiling. "I'd better hang back for a little while, like we figured—to make sure they don't re-discover their courage and show up for another try. You go ahead after that buggy. I'll be along in a short."

"Okay. But watch that pretty little ass of yours," J.D. said.

Now Kate grinned. "That's your job."

"Fair enough. You keep it in one piece, I'll gladly do my part."

They exchanged a quick kiss and then J.D. was off, pushing his horse hard once again in order to catch up with the fleeing buggy and try to bring their rescue attempt to a satisfactory conclusion.

◆◇◆

It worked in J.D.'s favor that the increasingly rugged terrain and the growing weariness of the pulling team had combined to slow the runaway considerably by the time he reached it.

What was working in nobody's favor, however, was the way the once broad, grassy, smoothly rounded hogback had become little more than a bare, rocky spine extending out over the gentler slopes and lush meadows of the valley below. To either side of the crest were now sheer, ragged drop-offs that meant almost certain death to any living thing unlucky enough to go over them.

J.D.'s horse sense told him there was the very real possibility that the wild-eyed, panicked team, instead of continuing on recklessly or slowing to a more controlled stop, might instead balk suddenly at these threatening surroundings and attempt a more abrupt halt. Such a move would surely flip or pitch the buggy wildly, sending it, its passengers—and most likely drag the horse team along, too—over the precarious drop-off.

12

J.D. figured he had only a matter of seconds to prevent such a catastrophe. As he closed on the buggy, he barely had room to fit alongside it without risking a misstep by his horse that would take both of them over the brink first. But he had complete faith in his mount, the big stallion having pulled him through scrapes as bad or worse than this in the past.

Drawing even with the fleeing team, J.D. saw the shortened lengths of what had once been reins flapping uselessly in the wind. As he'd guessed, they had been cut. That left only one way for him to play it.

Bracing himself, getting set, he leaned out from his saddle and then kicked free of the stirrups and launched himself onto the back of the nearest puller. He settled in place, strong thighs locking him there as his left fist immediately grabbed the bridle of the horse he was now astride and began drawing back. At the same time, he reached over with his right hand and did the same with the other half of the team.

"Whoa! Hold up now! Whoa there!"

Tired, scared, confused, the horses seemed almost to welcome the assured grip and voice of J.D. They slowed somewhat jerkily, but not too fast, and then came to a halt, blowing hard, shoulders muscles fluttering under foamy, sweat-drenched hides.

J.D. twisted around on his boldly attained perch and looked back at the buggy's two disheveled passengers, still braced rigidly against the crash they'd thought was inevitable.

Flashing an easy, reassuring grin, he said, "Everything okay back there, folks?"

Chapter 3

Assisting the buggy passengers down onto terra firma provided J.D. the chance to make a quick but thorough up-close appraisal of the pair.

The man looked to be in his middle to late fifties. Just under six feet in height, sturdy build, ruddy complexion, ruggedly handsome face framed by bristly sideburns that were pale yellow in color, made even paler by being shot through with flecks of gray. The matching jacket and trousers he wore fit too well to be anything but tailored and his shirt was of the finest material. He definitely appeared to be someone of wealth yet, at the same, the way he carried himself and the thick-fingered paw he thrust out to shake J.D.'s hand gave the impression of a man who'd also done a good deal of hard physical work in his time.

"You don't know how much I hate admitting I lost control of my own damn team," the man said as he pumped J.D.'s arm. "But thank Christ you came along when you did, young fella!"

"Just the luck of the draw that I happened to be in the neighborhood," J.D. replied.

Even as he was exchanging words with the man, J.D. couldn't keep his gaze from sliding over and drinking in a good, long look at his female companion. She was the kind of woman most men would have a hard time keeping their eyes off of. Twenty or so years younger than the man, with a finely chiseled face, sparkling green eyes, and a pile of lustrous auburn hair that had once been neatly piled atop her head but now was a bit wind-blown, she cut a fine figure of a woman by any standard.

J.D. really didn't have to study her at any great length to confirm all of this. As a matter of fact, he was already intimately familiar with her "fine figure" and all the rest. The only question was, since they were pretty far afield from where he'd known her in the past and she was now in the company of another man, he didn't know whether or not she would wish to acknowledge their prior acquaintance.

The question was quickly answered when those green eyes took on an extra twinkle and her generous mouth spread in a wide smile as she exclaimed, "J.D. Blaze, what an amazing and wonderful surprise to see you again!"

The woman spread her arms for a hug, but J.D. balked. "Jeez, Belle, I'm all sweaty and dusty here," he protested. "I wouldn't want to soil that fancy dress you got on."

"Like I haven't seen you sweaty plenty of times before. And as far as this dress, it would have gotten damaged far worse if those frenzied horses had taken us over a cliff the way it looked certain they were going to. Now step over here and give me a hug, damn it!"

Having the man standing right there—inasmuch as J.D. hadn't yet figured out exactly what the relationship between the two was—made the moment a little awkward. But, other than that, a command to embrace the red-haired beauty J.D. formerly knew as Belle Fenton could hardly be considered hardship duty. So J.D. stepped into it and gave her a good squeezing. The scent of what he remembered as being her favorite perfume filled his nostrils. And the contours of her, especially the warm pressure of breasts that had lost none of their firm fullness, were also well remembered. Disconcertingly so, in fact, being as he was now a married man.

When they stepped apart, Belle turned to the man in the tailored suit and said, smiling, "Darling, let me introduce you to J.D. Blaze, an old and dear friend of mine...And, J.D., please meet my husband, Oliver Braedon."

Once again the two men shook hands.

This time Braedon's grip was even firmer that before. He was smiling, too, as he said, "Pleased to meet you, Mr. Blaze. *Very* pleased, considering how you just saved our lives."

"Well, I don't know about that," J.D. said. "Those horses had a pretty good head of steam going, it's true, but there was still a chance they might have come to their senses and stopped before—"

"No offense, son," Braedon interrupted, "but that's bull-crap and you know it. Those panicked poor fools were hell bent on taking us to our doom and only your intervention prevented it. I'm grateful beyond words. If there's ever any-thing at any time I can do to repay you, all you have to do is name it."

"And those aren't just idle words," Belle was quick to add, a ring of both earnestness and pride in her voice. "My hus-band stands behind what he says. The name Braedon means a great deal around these parts, in case you didn't know, and Oliver's convictions and the courage and strength to back them up are big parts of the reason why."

"Okay. I'll be sure to keep that in mind," J.D. allowed.

Belle smiled again, this time with an impish twist. "Now that we've got that straight...Tell me, what are you doing galloping around in these mountains apart from riding to the rescue of those in need?"

"Really, Belle," her husband scolded. "Don't you think it's rather blunt and impertinent to grill the young man like—"

"Relax, Oliver," she cut him off. "I told you, J.D. and I are old friends. He wouldn't know what to think if I was anything less than blunt and impertinent. And, just to make things clear for you, J.D., Oliver knows all about my, shall we say, 'checkered past'. In fact, like you, he shared a slice of it with me. That's how we met. But none of that matters any longer. It's all behind us. Which gives you leave to speak freely and remove the strained expression from your face that makes you look like you swallowed a bug."

Although someone who was seldom caught at a loss for words, that's exactly how J.D. found himself when Belle finished saying her piece. He almost would have welcomed a bug to swallow, he told himself, as a distraction from just standing there groping for a response.

Luckily, a far better and *truly* welcome distraction showed up instead.

At the sound of approaching hoof beats, J.D. and the Braedons turned their heads to watch Kate riding at a gallop to join them. Her hat was pushed back off her head, though still retained by its neck string so that it bounced lightly between her shoulders and left her thick blonde hair streaming out full and rich behind her. And although she was an expert, graceful rider, moving as if she were an extension of the horse itself, there was still enough bounce to the gallop to cause her generous breasts to sway and jiggle enticingly.

A warm feeling swelled inside J.D., the way it always did, at the mere sight of her. Only this time, given his keen awareness of Kate's jealous nature and the fact that a former lover of his, in the curvaceous form of Belle Braedon, was standing right beside him...well, the warm feeling was accompanied by a queasy knot of anxiety low in his gut.

"Well, I'm glad to see you made it in time," Kate announced as she reined up in a swirl of dust.

"How did you make out?" J.D. said in return. "Any more trouble from those three hombres?"

Kate shook her head. "Not a peep. Way I figure it, they're still hightailing it into the tall and uncut."

"So you're also responsible for chasing that pack of howling coyotes off our tail?" Braedon said, apparently realizing for the first time that his former pursuers were no longer part of the picture.

"They were sorta in our way when we took out to try and catch up with your runaway team," J.D. explained. "We had to, er, bump 'em *out* of the way."

"Good for you! I hope you bumped the dirty bastards clean off the mountain!"

"Language, Oliver," Belle cautioned him. "There are ladies present...well, one anyway." She cut her gaze over to J.D. "Speaking of which, are you going to introduce us to your lovely accomplice, J.D.?"

"By all means," J.D. replied, trying to gauge the undercurrent running between Kate and Belle as they coolly made eye contact. With a bit of a flourish, he gestured to Kate and said, "This hard-riding, gun-toting beauty is Kate, my wife...Kate, darling, this is Belle and Oliver Braedon."

"Wait a minute!" Braedon said abruptly, excitedly. "Kate and J.D. Blaze—I recognize your names now. Of course! You're the married team of gunfighters who've been gaining such a reputation over the past couple of years. How could I not have seen it immediately?"

"Gunfighters?" Belle echoed, looking somewhat puzzled.

"That's right. Gunfighters! Two of the best in the West," her husband confirmed, excitement still ringing in his voice.

"Be that as it may," J.D. said, "right at the moment we're letting our gun barrels cool off a mite while we enjoy a few days' vacation here in Estes Valley."

"At least that was the general idea," Kate added. "We're staying at the Big Thompson Lodge in Elk City, you see, and rode out late this morning for a picnic. We had our spread laid out a ways back, a nice private spot on a slope overlooking a little waterfall. It was from there that we saw you, up on the crest, with your out of control team and those rowdies chasing you."

"We can thank our lucky stars," said Braedon, "that you were in a position where you were able—and willing—to intervene."

"Who were those three hellraisers, anyway? The men hoorahing you?" J.D. asked.

"Hold on a minute," said Belle, raising a hand. "The answer to that—and anything else you wish to know, since you've certainly earned the right—can be had. But surely we can find a more suitable time and place to continue with this, can we not?

"Since we clearly interrupted your picnic lunch, how about this: Oliver's ranch is only a few miles up the valley from your lodge. Let us send a driver and carriage for you this evening and you will be our guests for dinner. Please. No, I insist. Then we can cover everything left to discuss in a far more comfortable setting. What say you?"

J.D. and Kate exchanged glances. He couldn't be certain what all was running through that pretty little head of hers, but in her eyes he was pretty sure he saw a hint of being intrigued by the invitation.

"Very well," he said. "But on one condition, if I may."

"Of course," replied Braedon. "What is it?"

"The carriage you send to pick us up?" J.D. tipped his head to indicate the still-blowing team that stood in front of the buggy. "Give these nags a rest, and send some different, less high strung ones, okay?"

Chapter 4

"I have absolutely no trouble believing that red-haired floozy used to be a prostitute," Kate was saying. "What flabbergasts me is that there was ever a point where you felt you had to pay for sex and, when you did, a cheap tumble with the likes of her was what you put your money on."

J.D knew he had to be mighty careful how he replied. Since Kate already had her claws out, it wouldn't be acceptable to just say nothing. She'd keep digging until she got a response. But if he said the *wrong* thing, those claws might go straight for the jugular.

Taking a deep breath, gritting his teeth, J.D. said, "It was hardly a cheap tumble. Belle was working at one of the most exclusive brothels in San Francisco and was their most requested gal."

Instead of the claws, he got the fire shooting out of Kate's eyes. "Is that supposed to make me feel *better*, you horny jackass?"

J.D. held up his hands, palms out, as if to ward off the heat being aimed his way. Moments like these, he told himself (and not for the first time), the name Blaze certainly suited the love of his life. He wondered if her temper had been any cooler under her maiden name of Aragon.

This exchange between them was taking place in their suite at the Big Thompson Lodge. Outside, the long shadows of late afternoon had deepened into evening and now the soft golden glow of ornate lamps filled their quarters, somehow making the well appointed furnishings look all the finer.

The soft lighting somehow made Kate look finer, too, especially in the stylish, off-the-shoulder gown she had spent the afternoon selecting from the lodge's women's wear shop. This was quite a trick from J.D.'s perspective, considering how she always looked exquisite in his eyes. Under the circumstances, though, he dared not compliment her. He knew that any attempt at flattery, no matter how sincere, would only be viewed by her as a lame attempt to get back in better graces.

"The point I was trying to make," J.D. said in response to the *horny jackass* accusation, "is that I didn't find Belle in some back alley crib and I wasn't so lowdown that's where I went prowling to take care of my horniness."

"It all falls under the same heading, pal." In sharp contrast to the fire in her eyes, Kate's tone was like ice.

J.D. let his arms drop. "Fine. If that's gonna be your attitude, we'll forget the whole dinner thing. When the carriage arrives to pick us up, I'll make some kind of excuse and send it back empty."

"And let that redheaded rip think she intimidates me? No way." Kate set her jaw defiantly. "We're going to that dinner, I'm wearing this fancy damn dress that's practically cutting me in two, and I'm going to charm the ass off of everybody there—especially that delusional old fool who was addled enough to fall under the spell of Miss 'Most Requested Gal' and end up marrying her."

"Aw, come on. I liked Braedon. He impressed me as a tough, stubborn cattleman who worked hard to grow one of the largest spreads in the valley, yet hasn't let his nose get turned up by success and wealth."

"Yeah, he's a hard worker alright. I've seen the type. The kind of hard worker who likely had his wife working right at his side—on top of bearing and raising those four kids he told us about—getting turned into an old woman before her time then planted early. And now he's gone and married a new one, half his age, who'll reap the benefits."

J.D. scowled. "That's unfair, Kate. You have no way of knowing—"

His words were interrupted by a loud, insistent knock on the door.

Both J.D. and Kate glanced at the clock on the mantle. It was too early for the Braedon carriage to be arriving, and they weren't expecting any other callers.

The demeanor and body language of each of them changed instantly. No matter the differences they'd been airing before, now the overriding instincts of caution and preparedness took over and kicked everything else aside. In their line of work, it was the only way to survive.

Since they'd only recently finished getting dressed in their fineries for the upcoming dinner, neither had on their gun belt. But, out of habit, the weapons were close at hand. They unleathered their respective Colts almost in unison. Because he was closest to the door, J.D. stepped to answer it. Kate edged off to one side of the room.

Holding the Colt down at his side, J.D. stood off-center of the door and said, "Who is it?"

A deep, slightly muffled voice said from the other side, "Name's Ruckner. Sam Ruckner. I work out at the Braedon ranch."

"You bring the carriage?" J.D. asked.

"No. I got nothing to do with no carriage. But I got an important message...from Mrs. Braedon."

"*Mrs.* Braedon?"

"That's right. There's been some trouble out at the ranch. Bad trouble. Mrs. Braedon gave me a note, said to ride hard as I could and get it to you."

J.D. glanced over at Kate. Her expression was unreadable except for maybe a slight pinch of concern.

"The door's unlocked," J.D. said to the man who'd called himself Ruckner. "Come ahead on in...Easy."

The door opened and Ruckner entered. He was a wiry, weathered looking gent of average height. Well north of fifty. Beard stubble, bushy walrus mustache, and clothes showing a good deal of wear and tear typical for ranch work. He held a battered, high-crowned hat in his hands and the mud-colored hair on the back of his head stood up in a cowlick from the hat's removal. His eyes made a sweep around the room, lingered for a moment on the vision of Kate, who held her pistol down so it was hidden behind the folds of her skirt, then finished their sweep and came to rest on J.D.

"Always wondered what it was like inside this place. Really something, ain't it?"

"That it is," allowed J.D., continuing to hold his own gun down at his side. "You mentioned a note?"

From his breast pocket, Ruckner withdrew a folded piece of paper and held it out. There was a rust-colored streak on the paper.

"That stain is blood—the blood of Oliver Braedon," Ruckner said in a voice lower and huskier than it had been a moment earlier.

J.D.'s eyes jumped to the man's face. Kate moved forward in hurried steps.

"What happened?" J.D. wanted to know.

"Mr. Braedon got shot."

"How seriously?" said Kate.

Ruckner's brow furled and his eyes turned watery. "Bad. Real bad. Two rifle rounds. I-I'm afraid he ain't gonna make it. But that ain't for me to say...I met the doctor heading out as I was coming into town."

Kate said, "Read what the note says, J.D."

Her husband shook open the paper. Words ran across it in a woman's flowery scrawl.

J.D. –

Please come at once.

I know I haven't any right to ask,

but there's no one else I can trust.

Oliver has been shot. I fear he may be dead

by the time you read this.

If it comes to that, I have reason

to also fear for myself.

— Belle

Chapter 5

The main house at the Braedon ranch was a long, low, sprawling affair constructed of timber and stone, set slightly off-center amidst numerous outbuildings, cattle pens, and corrals. The outlying structures were mostly just murky shapes in the starlit night, but the house itself was awash in soft yellow illumination pouring out of its many windows and from lanterns hanging on the posts of the canopied front porch.

J.D. and Kate followed Ruckner out from the town and rode with him to the hitch rails directly in front of the big house. There was a half dozen or so people milling on the grass and on the porch near what appeared to be the main entrance. One of the persons on the porch was a woman in a long, plain dress. She was holding a handkerchief near her face. Standing close to her was a younger girl, about twelve or so, in a short-skirted dress and with her hair in pigtails. The rest were all men clad in standard range clothes.

The three new arrivals dismounted, tied their horses, and walked toward the front door. J.D. and Kate had traded their dinner garb for more customary outfits—trousers and a boiled collarless shirt for J.D., split riding skirt and blouse for Kate. Both had their guns strapped on and in prominent display. As they passed through the men on the grass, J.D. could feel the weight of their eyes and it hardly felt like a welcoming pat on the back. When they climbed the steps to the front porch, the woman standing there turned and looked away.

Inside, in a spacious parlor beyond a rather cramped foyer, more people milled. In the center of the room, a semi circle of five men stood with their backs to the foyer, focusing intently on something directly in front of them that their shoulder-to-shoulder positioning obscured. Sitting on a high-backed armchair just off to the left of the men, was an ashen-faced Belle Braedon.

At the sight of Ruckner and the Blazes entering, Belle rose to her feet. This reaction from her, along with the sound of the entrants' muffled footfalls on the rich carpeting, caused the lineup of men to shift and some of them to turn part way around. Through this separation of bodies, J.D. could then see the form of Oliver Braedon lying motionless on a couch. The front of his shirt was yanked open and there were smears of bright crimson on both clothing and flesh. A small, frail-looking, gray-haired man was perched on a footstool directly at his side, leaning intently over the prone man. An open medical bag rested on the floor next to him. Next to the bag sat a pan of bloody water.

As Belle started forward, a tall, stocky man stepped away from the others and made an obvious move to get in front of her, effectively blocking her advance.

"Who are these people?" the stocky man said.

"They're friends of mine, Clay," Belle answered. "I asked Ruckner to bring them here."

J.D. immediately noted the lack of force in her tone. Not at all like the Belle he knew.

Clay fixed Ruckner with a disapproving look. He was a ruddy-faced individual, what some might consider handsome in a rugged kind of way. But, in concert with fleshy jowls starting to form under the hinges of his jaw and the beginning bulge of a pot gut that pushed out below the dangling tails of a bright green string tie, he also had the look of a man on the brink of going to seed from soft living and maybe too much alcohol. J.D. decided he looked like a younger, softer version of Oliver Braedon and the similar pale yellow coloring of his thick sideburns and a headful of wavy hair pretty much solidified the hunch.

"You bring strangers here, at a time like this, without bothering to mention it to *me*?" Clay demanded of Ruckner.

Ruckner held his ground, not backing up from the bigger man's glare. "Like Mrs. Braedon said, she asked me. I didn't figure there needed to be any more to it."

"Well, you figured wrong. You work for me, not her."

Ruckner's eyes narrowed. "I ride for the Braedon brand. The Bar OB. You might give me day-to-day orders, Clay, but your dad is still he-goose of the operation, and when his wife asks me to do something then I reckon that's about as far up the order chain as I need to go."

Clay Braedon's glare turned threatening. His already ruddy face reddened more deeply and his fists balled. He looked almost ready to take a swing at Ruckner.

But the doctor spoke up, stopping him. "Clay," he said, his voice surprisingly deep and strong in contrast to his slight build. "If there ever was an appropriate time for your customary belligerence, it's certainly not now."

The medico stood up and turned to face those gathered about him. His gaze skimmed each in turn and then settled on Belle and Clay. "I'm sorry...I did everything I could...But he's gone."

A stunned, dumbfounded look seemed to grip every face in the room.

Clay Braedon muttered something under his breath, something so hushed that J.D. couldn't hear it well enough to understand from less than three feet away.

Belle, who had remained partially behind Clay ever since

he blocked her way, now went very rigid and motionless in her stance. She squeezed her eyes tightly shut. After a moment, a single tear leaked out and ran down her cheek.

The eyes of the men who remained standing by the couch where now only the corpse of Oliver Braedon lay, had shifted to focus on Clay. None of them bothered to even glance in the direction of the dead man's widow.

Somewhat surprisingly, it was Kate who went to her. Taking Belle gently by the arm, she turned her to one side and said, "Come on, honey, let's step into another room for a minute." Over her shoulder, she said to the collection of distracted men, "Somebody get me a glass of water for her, maybe even some brandy."

The doctor responded, saying, "Yes. That's an excellent idea." He pointed to a set of double doors against one wall and said to Kate, "There's a study through there. Take her in and have her sit down, my dear. I'll be in shortly."

"You go ahead with them," Ruckner said to J.D. "I'll bring some water and brandy."

J.D. did as the helpful wrangler suggested. He held the door for Kate and Belle and the three of them entered into what the doctor had called a study. It was a room about half the size of the one they'd just quit, furnished to masculine tastes, all dark wood and leather.

Kate directed Belle to a massive chair covered in cowhide.

J.D. closed the door behind them and stood for a minute regarding the two women. He'd known all along that Kate's sharp-tongued remarks about Belle back at the lodge, after he had filled her in on his past with the attractive redhead, had come strictly from blind jealousy, not anything personal. That was one of the few areas where his lovely wife tended to let her harsher emotions override her otherwise cool reasoning.

When Ruckner showed up with the news that Oliver

Braedon had been shot, the more level-headed, compassionate Kate had promptly come to the fore. When pressed by J.D. as to why she was so willing for them to respond to Belle's request for help, the terse response had been, "Don't be ridiculous. We didn't go to all the trouble of saving her and her husband's backsides this afternoon only to stand by and allow them to end up getting shot anyway!"

And so it was. The care and attention Kate was showing to Belle now was Kate continuing to be compassionate and protective. Which wasn't to say that later, when whatever the Blaze team was about to become involved in had reached some kind of conclusion and it was just the two of them alone at some point, the love of J.D.'s life might very well remember to be jealous all over again and pepper him with a new flurry of uncharitable remarks about his conquests prior to meeting her.

In the meantime, there was the grim business at hand to deal with.

J.D. walked over and put hand on Belle's shoulder. "Do you feel up to talking about it?" he asked.

"Of course. I must," Belle said, wiping the wetness from her cheek with the back of one hand.

"Just take your time," encouraged Kate.

Belle began to speak, soft and steady, her voice basically a flat monotone. Her gaze was fixed straight ahead, seeing something beyond the walls of the room. "It was late in the afternoon. The sun was just beginning to set. Oliver had bathed and shaved but, before getting dressed for our dinner, he went out to the carriage shed to check with the young man he had slated to drive into town and pick you two up.

"The lad's name is Jorge, you see, and he's the son of the lady who has cooked and cleaned house here for years. Her husband, Jorge's father, used to be a wrangler for Oliver but was killed in a horse fall. So the boy grew up viewing Oliver as a sort of surrogate father. I'm afraid it's made him feel a little privileged and causes him to think he can get away with being lazy some of the time. He's an excellent teamster, but can be lax about other chores. That's why Oliver went to check on him, to make sure he'd given the carriage a good cleaning and adequately groomed the horses." Belle paused and the corners of her mouth lifted ever so faintly, remembering, before she added, "Oliver was quite taken with you two. He wanted to make a good impression."

"He'd already accomplished that," J.D. assured her. Even Kate, before her jealous rant picked up a full head of steam, had remarked how genuine and easily likable Oliver Braedon had seemed.

"On his way back to the house," Belle continued, "was when someone used a rifle to shoot Oliver from concealment. They fired twice, rapidly, and hit him both times high in the chest. Just above his heart. It's a dreadful shame that Jorge had to be the first one to reach him, even though several others heard the shots. The boy is devastated. Still, he had the presence of mind to notice a haze of gunsmoke over on the back side of the small corral just to the north of our house, near where Oliver had been walking. Sheriff Walburton determined that the angle the bullets went in matched with someone firing from that spot."

"So the sheriff has already done some investigating into this?" J.D. asked.

Belle nodded. "That's right. He came right away when word reached town. He got here a little while ahead of Doc Beedle."

"Then he's one of the men out in the other room?"

"Yes. Him and his chief deputy, young Walt Early."

"We already got introduced, in a manner of speaking, to your charming stepson Clay," said Kate. "Who was the other young man standing by the couch when we came in?"

"That's Curtis. Oliver's youngest son. He still lives here at home, as does Nora, Oliver's daughter."

"There was a woman and a girl of about twelve or so on the front porch when we got here. Was one of them Nora?"

Belle shook her head. "No. That was Clay's wife, Marjorie, and their daughter Roslyn. They have their own place, just across the way. Nora and Chuck, the middle son, have been gone most of the day helping a neighbor round up and brand some cattle. They've been sent for, of course." She gave another shake of her head. "I'm surprised they aren't here yet...though I can't say I'm looking forward to their presence when they do arrive."

"Why's that?" Kate wanted to know.

"They take too closely after their big brother Clay. Passionate, I guess some would call it. Simply hot-headed is more the way I'd put it. You saw just a small example...Curtis is the only one of the children who's not so volatile." Belle's shoulders lifted and fell in a fatalistic shrug. "At any rate, they'll all take turns at being devastated by their father's passing. And sincerely so, don't get me wrong...But then, inevitably, their focus will shift to me."

J.D. frowned. "You said in your note that, if Oliver died, you feared for yourself. From them—his three children—did you mean?"

"They surely do not like me. They've made that crystal clear," Belle stated. "But that's only part—"

She was cut short by the arrival of Ruckner. He gave a cursory tap on the door and then came on in without waiting. In one hand he held a glass of water, in the crook of an elbow he clenched a decanter of amber liquid with a second glass turned upside down over the snout. He heeled the door shut behind him.

Marching over to Belle, he said, "Here you go, Mrs. Braedon. Name your poison—the water or the brandy."

Belle reached for the water. Ruckner placed the brandy on a lamp stand next to her chair.

"Actually," Belle said after taking a sip, "I wasn't thinking clearly when the doctor suggested we come in here. In that cabinet"—she pointed—"Oliver already has a modest stock of liquor. Some brandy and whiskey, I know, probably some wine. I'm sure there are glasses, too. Please help yourselves if you wish."

J.D. and Kate declined. Ruckner poised uncertainly, his gaze shifting back and forth between Belle and the liquor cabinet.

"That includes you, too, Sam," Belle told him.

The old wrangler hesitated no longer. He went to the cabinet, poured himself a generous slug of whiskey and threw it down with a practiced flourish. Passing the back of one hand across his mouth, he said, "Oh yeah, prime stuff. Obliged, ma'am. I'll go on back out in the other room now, so you folks can talk. But I'll be right outside the door if you need me."

"Thank you, Sam. Let me know when Nora and Chuck arrive, please."

"I'll do that." Then, muttering under his breath as he made his way out the door, Ruckner added, "Don't hardly expect there'll be any way to miss it."

When he was gone and had closed the door behind him once more, Belle said, "Apart from Oliver, of course, Sam and young Curtis are about the only two people I've grown to feel comfortable around since coming here."

"How long has that been?" Kate asked.

"Ten months. Sam and I married in San Francisco, honeymooned on a sailing cruise up and down the coast, then he brought me home to meet the family." A corner of Belle's mouth lifted wryly. "To say I came as something of a shock

32

to them would be an understatement for the ages."

"So they've been against you from the start?"

Belle frowned thoughtfully. "I don't know if 'against me' is the right term, at least not right away. More like they weren't *in favor* of me, not as a wife for their father. I think that would have been true for any woman he chose to marry. Dorothy—Oliver's first wife, and mother to all of the children—has been dead for nearly four years now. But no one seemed prepared to consider that Oliver, even going on sixty, was still a healthy, virile man who could have needs."

"Do they know about your, er, past?" asked J.D.

"No. Oliver and I decided, before we ever wed, that should the truth ever come out—such as encountering someone like you, J.D., who recognized me from those days—we would neither hide from nor try to deny it. But, by the same token, we would be understandably discreet and not broadcast it, either, if we didn't have to...God, that's all I'd need is for my past to come out now."

J.D. said, "It goes without saying, I trust, that you have no concern in that regard from Kate or me."

"Of course. I know that."

"A moment ago," Kate said, "you resisted saying Oliver's children were against you, but then added 'at least not right away'. Did something subsequent happen to make you think their feelings toward you have grown more aggressive?"

Belle took another sip of her water, and when she lowered the glass her mouth twisted as if the taste had been bitter. "Yes. The damn will. What had been a tense but manageable situation turned really mean and ugly after Oliver let it be known he had modified his will."

Before continuing, Belle set the water aside and poured herself a splash of the brandy. "You see, Oliver planned on building a new house for just the two of us on some scenic high ground about a mile from the ranch headquarters here. After we'd moved, in the event of his death, the will modification stipulated that the new house and ten surrounding acres would be strictly mine."

"That doesn't sound so unfair or unreasonable," Kate commented.

"It was still enough to ruffle some feathers, even though the rest of what had been drawn up after Dorothy's passing stayed basically as it was." Belle held up a slim index finger. "Except for one added proviso—namely, that I would also receive ten percent of the profits earned from all ranch operations, payable to me quarterly."

J.D. smiled crookedly. "Aha. Now we're talking money yanked directly out of the kiddies' pockets. And nothing brings the venom and true character out of a loving family more than when survivors start clawing to make sure nobody else gets a share of the will they think rightfully ought to be theirs."

Kate scowled. "If everything would otherwise have been split evenly between the four kids—twenty-five percent four ways, in other words—then the modification allotting ten percent to Belle would only amount to each of them giving up two and a half percent. That's hardly a severe cut to anybody."

"You're applying logic, with no room for emotion or plain old greed," J.D. pointed.

"Greedy like spoiled little brats, the way it sounds to me," grumbled Kate.

Belle drained the brandy she had poured. "At any rate, that's the way it stands...Or, rather, that's the way it *stood*, before Oliver got killed. I've little reason to expect his passing will suddenly reverse their opinions of me."

"What about that? Oliver's killing, I mean—his shooting," said J.R. "Do you suspect one of his kids were upset enough over his changing of the will to be behind that?"

"Oh, God," Belle groaned. "No, I can't bring myself to believe such a thing as that. No matter what else, each and every one of them loved their father. Besides, what would killing Oliver gain any of them? The will is already in place."

J.D. made a sour face. "I've known plenty of people who supposedly loved somebody they ended up killing. Sometimes in plain awful ways. Heck, there was this old gal once—a mother and grandmother, she was, married and totally devoted from all outward appearances to the same fella for thirty-five years. One evening, nobody was ever sure why, while he was sitting at the kitchen table waiting for her to serve supper, she came up behind him with a heavy old iron skillet full of hot grease and—"

"J.D.!" Kate cut him short. "I'm pretty sure you made your point. Further details, no matter how cheerful or entertaining, really aren't necessary."

Belle looked relieved. Catching sight of that, J.D. shrugged off his disappointment over not being able to finish his story, and said, "Okay, if that's the way you feel about it."

"It is," Kate assured him. Then, turning her focus to Belle, she said, "It seems to me that a more obvious line of questioning should be about those three riders who were hoorahing your buggy ride earlier today. They clearly were out to harm your husband or you. Or both. Any idea who they were? And could they be behind the shooting here this evening?"

Belle made a groaning sound again. She reached for the brandy and poured some more. Lifting the glass to her mouth but not taking a drink, she said softly, "Yes...and yes."

Chapter 6

Further discussion of the mystery riders who had already shown dangerous intentions on at least one prior occasion, was delayed by the arrival of Nora and Chuck Braedon. Now that all members were present, family obligations—no matter how strained—warranted Belle's presence once again in the parlor. And since she made it clear she wasn't ready to talk about the riders in front of anyone else, Kate and J.D. had little choice but to put the matter on hold until they had another chance to be alone with her.

Despite all the anxiety over hard feelings and volatile tempers, the meeting in the parlor was subdued, respectful, and productive as far as reaching necessary decisions about how to proceed in regard to funeral arrangements for the deceased patriarch. Nora's only contribution was to sob softly throughout, comforted by a misty-eyed, equally quiet Curtis. The two older sons, Clay and Chuck, stood stoically and spoke in low, measured tones. Belle held her own, commenting sparingly, occasionally dabbing away tears with the aid of a handkerchief provided her by the doctor.

It was decided that the body, which had been shrouded and temporarily moved to a side room, would be taken by wagon that night to the undertaker in Elk City. In the morning, everyone would assemble again, in the town, and finalize remaining details with Reverend Melker, the Baptist minister who served the family's religious needs.

When Belle stated she wished to accompany the body to

town but not return to the house any more that night, no one objected. When Kate extended an invitation for her to stay over with them in their suite at the lodge, Belle did not hesitate to accept.

J.D. recognized the practical side to this, inasmuch as it would provide the privacy for them to finish where they'd left off, but he couldn't decide if that was the only reason Kate made the offer or if there was more. The love of his life could be headstrong and hot-tempered and certainly quick to display jealousy. But, J.D. reminded himself, she could also be very compassionate. In any case, having Belle spend the night with them didn't seem like a bad idea.

With that agreed to and assurances from the sheriff that he and his deputy would accompany Belle to town and make sure she got to the Big Thompson Lodge okay, the Blazes saw fit to take their leave. While their presence had been tolerated, other than the initial reaction from Clay when they first showed up, it was nevertheless a time best left to family and those closest to the deceased. Even Belle likely would appreciate some reflective moments to herself, plus she would need the chance to pack an overnight bag and otherwise prepare while the wagon and body were being readied for the trip. J.D. and Kate had some things to hash over, just between themselves, as well.

It felt good to get out of the crowded house and back into the fresh mountain air. The night was crisp and cool, silver-shot with illumination from the moon and stars, and the scent of high country pine filled their nostrils as they rode at an easy gait away from the ranch headquarters.

"One thing is for sure," J.D. commented. "Whatever else it looks like we're getting ourselves involved in, the biggest danger might turn out to be the risk of starving to death."

"How do you figure that?" Kate asked.

"Look at the record. Our picnic lunch earlier today got interrupted by the runaway buggy. Now the big, fancy dinner we were figuring on tonight clearly ain't gonna happen thanks to a murderous ambush...Can't you see the pattern? If I don't eat pretty soon, I may be too weak to lift my six-gun in case any shootin' trouble pops up."

Kate rolled her eyes. "Lord. The way you carry on...If you're lucky, maybe we'll get attacked by a mountain lion or something on the trail, while you still have the strength to draw your gun and shoot it. Then we can stop to cook the beast over a campfire, eat it, and you'll be nourished enough to make it the rest of the way to town."

"Right about now," J.D. replied, "that don't sound half bad."

They rode for a ways in silence. Until Kate said, "What you said back there a minute ago—about what we're getting ourselves involved in. Is it a done deal, then? *Are* we going to stay involved?"

J.D. frowned. "I thought we'd pretty much decided that when we came in response to Belle's note. As I recall, you said something to the effect that we didn't go to all the trouble of saving the Braedons like we did only to have them go ahead and come to harm anyway."

"I know what I said. Trouble is, they got harmed regardless. Oliver shot to death, Belle possibly still in danger. I don't like that worth a damn."

"Me neither," J.D. agreed. "I mean, it's not like we *signed on* to protect them or anything. But all the same..."

"Still, we need to remember that our help and involvement may not be welcomed by everybody," Kate pointed out.

"Ain't hardly like we haven't mixed in plenty of other situations where we weren't welcomed by all sides. Hell, it's kinda what we do," J.D. reminded her.

"But usually get paid for."

"True," J.D. conceded. "But we both know we don't take jobs that are *just* about the money...In this case, there's only one thing that matters to me: Considering the past between Belle and me, are you sure you want to stick with this, protecting her and all, and trying to help get to the bottom of who killed Oliver and why?"

Kate didn't answer right away. She slowed her horse.

"I'll tell you right now," J.D. added, "I'm inclined to want to try and help her. Maybe for old time's sake, maybe just because I see her as somebody in a tight who ain't got many friends around she can count on. But if you ain't fully comfortable with it, if it'll put a strain between you and me, then there's no way—"

"Save the rest," Kate stopped him, "or I'll start to think thou doest protest too much."

J.D. look bewildered. "Say again?"

"Never mind. Just accept that you've made your point. I, too, am inclined to want to help your former floozy of a girlfriend."

"Not a real enthusiastic way of putting it."

"Well, it's the best you're going to get. Much as I wasn't prepared to like her, I've got to admit I've come around some. It's plenty clear she doesn't have many people pulling for her, and you know what a sucker I am for an underdog. What's more, in the face of it all, she's showing guts. And I like that in anybody." Kate turned her head and nailed J.D. with a narrow-eyed glare. "But if it turns out she's got guts enough to try and rekindle some sputtering old flame between the two of you...then I'll shoot her myself."

Chapter 7

The first shot ripped apart the night and, in the same instant, the slug *whapped!* against a corral post three inches from the side of J.D.'s face. Chips of whitewash and wood slivers spat against his cheek. Acting with lightning-fast reflexes, J.D. pitched himself back and down, twisting to sweep his left arm behind him in a motion that sent Kate also sprawling.

Together, they hit the straw-strewn ground of the shadowy aisle running between rows of tidy horse stalls. Kate immediately rolled one way, J.D. the other. Before they stopped rolling, their hands had blurred to the holsters at their waists and came up with drawn Colts.

By then, more shots were sizzling through the horse barn of the Big Thompson Lodge. Additional rounds smacked into posts and rails, others gouged low into the dirt. All were concentrated with deadly purpose, peppering the immediate area where J.D. and Kate had hit the deck.

But the intended targets knew better than to stay where they'd last been seen. Alternately rolling, crawling, and scrambling on hands and knees—between horses' legs and sometimes through deposits of manure, no matter how tidy those stalls looked from the outside—the Blaze team spread out quickly, aiming to keep from showing themselves again until they were better positioned. Had the ambushers been smarter, they might have held their fire momentarily in order to try and track their quarry's movement by sound.

But they were too eager for that. Pouring on more lead seemed to be their entire strategy.

J.D. scooted in behind a pile of gunnysacks packed with oats. He removed his hat and peered cautiously out through a gap between two of the sacks, Colt raised and ready as he made a quick appraisal of his and Kate's situation.

The shots kept coming, but they were nowhere close to where he now was. The horses in the stalls were getting more and more agitated, snorting nervously, kicking against their confines, a few emitting shrill sounds of alarm.

The barn was a long rectangular structure with a corral outside on the back end and a set of wide double doors at the front, facing out toward the main part of the lodge. The double doors were propped open in deference to the clear summer night. The lane that led up to the lodge was lined with low-burning lanterns mounted on poles. Illumination from these, combined with more pouring down from the nighttime sky, shone for a ways into the barn. Beyond that limited reach of light, however, everything else quickly melted into a crazy-quilt pattern of gray blotches, deepening shadows, and stark blackness.

J.D. wished he could call out to Kate—one, to make sure she was okay; two, to gain some sense of where she'd scrambled to. But that would only give away his position and, if she were reckless enough to reply (for which she was too smart), hers as well.

The other thought that raced through J.D.'s mind was speculation on why Kate hadn't returned fire yet. It meant either she wasn't able to, or that she was waiting for him to make the first move. The latter was more or less standard procedure developed from past similar situations...Although it wasn't like Kate to hold patiently for very long.

So okay. If it was up to him to open the ball for their side, then J.D. was damn sure up to the task.

There were three shooters firing on them. Not that it necessarily mattered, but it seemed logical to figure it was the same three from this morning. One of them—the one who'd fired first, by J.D.'s reckoning—was positioned just outside the double doors at the front, off to the right and behind a large wooden rain barrel. A second one was near the rear of the barn, lost in a wall of blackness except for his recurring muzzle flashes. The third was up in a narrow loft that hung cantilevered out over the side of the building opposite from J.D.—the side Kate had scrambled toward. Assuming she'd stayed over there, that meant the third shooter was somewhere above her. The good news was that he couldn't shoot down on her, but neither did she have any better angle for firing up at him.

The flip side to that was the fact J.D. *did* have a decent angle on the loft shooter—and vice versa. The trick would be for J.D. to make it count if he opened up on the ambushing buzzard, with only a muzzle flash at an upward angle to aim for. His return fire from that vantage point, if he didn't score an immediate hit, would put him at a real disadvantage because having the cover of merely being *behind* something wouldn't do him a hell of a lot of good with bullets coming at him from above.

But J.D. hadn't lasted doing gun work for this long without possessing the nerve to take a chance and also having learned a trick or three along the way.

He got himself set, extending his gun hand out at arm's length in the direction of the shooter behind the rain barrel. But his real concentration, via peripheral vision, was on the shooter in the loft. As soon as the latter fired off another round at where J.D. *wasn't,* the gunfighter triggered two quick shots at the rain barrel, revealing where he'd made it to instead. An instant after the Colt did its double buck in his fist, he pitched himself to the opposite end of the gunnysack pile from where his hand had been when he fired. This put him a full five feet away from the muzzle flashes the high ambusher would now be swinging his aim toward.

When the first bullet sizzled down, blasting open one of the oat sacks, J.D. was ready. He fanned three rapid-fire shots at a spot six inches above where he'd seen flame licking out of a gun barrel. One or more of the slugs hit true. J.D. heard his target emit a strangled cry and then a murky shape came hurtling out and down through the alternating bands of lighter-darker shadows until it crashed heavily to the ground.

That was one ambusher taken care of. But it still left two others, very much alive and now re-focused with heightened intensity on what J.D. had revealed to be his new location. As he hunkered low behind the oat sacks, thumbing fresh loads into his Colt, a flurry of shots hammered his cover. Puffs of dust spurted up like miniature geysers and streams of oats started pouring out, rattling softly, released through the bullet holes.

It was at this point—exactly as J.D. had been expecting and counting on—that Kate joined the party.

J.D. heard the familiar report of her Colt, issuing a set of rapid-fire blasts almost identical to the series he'd unloaded on the loft shooter. Before J.D. had time to look around, he heard the pained yelp from the rear of the barn, followed quickly by the thump of another body hitting the dirt. The shooting from back there stopped...permanently, J.D. was confident.

The shooting from behind the rain barrel stopped, too. With the odds suddenly turned against him, the ambusher out there was clearly having some serious thoughts about continuing what he and his comrades had started.

Into the lull, J.D. called to Kate. "How you doing over there, love of my life?"

"Fine, now," she replied. "I thought you were never going to cut loose on that jasper I could hear clumping around above me. I was starting to worry you might be hurt."

"Nah, I was just funnin' with this sorry lot, letting 'em think they might have a chance against us," J.D. told her. "I had the one at the rear spotted by his muzzle flash for a lot longer than he deserved to keep living. My trigger finger was getting mighty itchy."

"Well, it stands at one apiece. How about the one who's left? You want to draw straws for him, or should we just go ahead and blast the hell out of him together?"

Kate chuckled. "Maybe we should let him choose."

"How about it, you bushwhackin' sonofabitch?" J.D. called out. "You mean to finish making a fight of this? Or you gonna yellow-out and end it with your guns thrown down?"

There was no answer. The only sound was the soft rattle of the oats still pouring out through the bullet holes in the gunnysacks.

Chapter 8

"And that was it? You just let him get away?" Sheriff Amos Walburton's heavy scowl hadn't left his face for the past half hour. It was hard to tell, however, if it was from disappointment, anger, or suspicion.

"We didn't *let* him get away," J.D. argued. "He took off on us while we were talking...sort of comparing notes, you might say...right after we'd cut down the other two. If you look out there, past that barrel he was hiding behind, you'll see it's all uncut soft grass. We had no way of hearing his footfalls to let us know he'd lit out, otherwise we would have given chase. Off in some trees we found the tied horses that must've belonged to the pair we shot, but the third ambusher was long gone."

"That matches with what the front desk clerk at the lodge reported," said Walt Early, the sheriff's deputy. "He—the desk clerk, that is—came running out at the sound of all the shooting and—"

"*Running* out?" Walburton questioned acidly.

"That's the way he said it." Early shrugged. "If he had any smarts, I imagine he came out a little cautiously. Anyway, right after the shooting lagged, he said, he saw a man duck out from behind that big rain barrel and run away off to the west."

"When we heard the clerk coming down from the lodge," Kate explained, "is when we first realized the remaining ambusher out there had taken flight."

Kate, J.D., the two lawmen, and Belle Braedon were gathered in the Blazes' suite at the lodge. An hour had passed since the ambush down at the horse barn. Walburton and Early—accompanying, as promised, the body of Oliver Braedon and his grieving widow on the wagon trip from the ranch—had shown up about a half hour after the shooting was over.

Repairing to the suite had been a way to gain some privacy for their subsequent discussion, to get away from the display of freshly dead bodies (mostly for Belle's sake), and to allow Kate and J.D. the chance to clean up a bit after scrambling for their lives on the floor of the horse barn.

"What a night," the sheriff lamented now, as he clamped a palm to the back of his neck and squeezed the knots of tension forming there. "In just a handful of hours, we've got shootings and knifings and dead bodies scattered from Hell to breakfast."

"I'm sure I speak for the Widow Clemens as well as myself," Belle responded coolly, "when I express our deep regret for how much the murders of our husbands must add to your inconveniences."

Walburton's face reddened around his scowl. "Please, Mrs. Braedon. Surely you know I didn't mean it that way."

When lanterns had been lighted throughout the horse barn to help facilitate the investigation into what had occurred there, a third body—in addition to the two shot by J.D. and Kate—had been discovered. It was identified as that of a young man named Virgil Clemens, who worked as a wrangler and stable hand for the lodge. He was found in an empty stall with his throat cut. According to his wife, he was working late to care for a sick horse. As a result, he evidently was happened upon by the ambushers when they arrived to lie in wait for the Blazes and subsequently killed to silence him from giving anything away.

"Your husband was a fine man and young Clemens was one of the most likable fellas in town," the sheriff continued. "Losing them is a tragedy for our whole valley. It's my job to try and keep things like that from happening around here, and it's a responsibility I don't take lightly...I hope you can pardon me if, in my anger and frustration, I spoke carelessly."

Belle sighed, her tone thawing. "Of course, Sheriff. I know you and Oliver were friends from way back. I'm sorry I snapped at you like that."

Walburton shook his head. "No need to be sorry. The stress and grief you're suddenly burdened with makes it perfectly understandable...What's less understandable," he added after a moment's pause, "is the question of whether or not the rifleman out at the ranch earlier and the ambushers here at the lodge are connected in some way."

"What connection could there be, Sheriff?" said J.D. "There was little similarity to the way the ambushes were set up, and the targets were certainly different."

"But there's still a common element to both," Deputy Early pointed out. "No offense, but that would be you and your wife. First, you were scheduled to show up out at the Braedon ranch for dinner. Then, obviously, you'd be coming back here to the stable and lodge once you returned from the Bar OB."

"That's pretty slim commonality, if you ask me," said Kate.

"And as far as the Blazes being invited to dinner," Belle added, "only a very few people even knew about that."

Early spread his hands. "Just making an observation, ma'am."

"All I know," said Walburton, "is that two murders in one night—and that's discounting the pair of ambushers you two shot, which I'm willing to write off as self defense—is something I damn sure don't want to spread any farther."

J.D. mustered up his own scowl. "Well, now. It's mighty big of you to 'write off' us blasting those two bushwhackers as 'self defense'. What the hell else would you call it? You know, Sheriff, you got a real knack for putting things in a way that a body could take exception to without trying very hard."

"You're talking to an officer of the law, mister. You'd better ease up a little there," advised Early.

J.D.'s nostrils flared. "I don't like being accused of something unfounded, that's all. And I like it even less when it comes in a smarmy, beating-around-the-bush kind of way. If somebody's got something to say to me, say it straight out."

"You want it straight?" the sheriff said. "Okay, here it is: Just because I didn't catch on to your names right away out at the ranch, don't mean I can't put one and one together when the bullets start flying and add it up to who you two really are. The notorious man-and-wife gunfighting duo, the Blazes. Wherever and whenever you show up, the spent cartridges and corpses start piling up in a hurry, ain't that right?"

"So what if it is?" Kate snapped back. "We never went out of our way to deny that or make it a secret. We even used our real names on the lodge register. But we came here strictly on vacation—a long overdue honeymoon, if you must know. And we never went for our guns until that pack of curly wolves tried to blow our brains out!"

"Maybe so," Walburton allowed. "And maybe it's nothing out of the ordinary, for you two, to have men come gunning for you in order to try and settle past differences."

One corner of J.D.'s mouth lifted in a thin smile. "Actually, it is. You see, folks we have serious differences with usually ain't left in any condition to show up again at all."

"So, having had a good look at the two men you killed to-night, you're still sure you never ran into either of them before?"

"We already answered that. No."

Walburton turned to Belle. "I'm sorry to have to ask you this again, ma'am—just like I was sorry to've had to ask you to look at them in the first place, out there in the barn—but you're sure you didn't recognize anything about those men, either?"

"Not a thing."

"With all due respect, ma'am, I can't help but ask you one more thing." The sheriff gestured toward the Blazes. "How it is, I wonder, you've chosen such violence prone friends?"

"Sometimes," Belle replied, "circumstances make those kinds of decisions for us. J.D. and I became friends a long time ago, in another place and at another time, when we both were leading rather different lives. Earlier today, strict-ly by coincidence, we encountered each other again while he and his wife were out enjoying a picnic and Oliver and I happened by on a buggy ride. Somehow it didn't occur to me to get clearance from the local law before inviting the two of them to dinner."

If there'd been any doubt, the way Belle blatantly avoided the rest of the details associated with that "buggy ride" made it plenty clear she still had reasons for holding back.

"And under the circumstances," Belle went on, "I consid-er running into each other again today to be my good for-tune. No matter your opinion of the Blazes, Sheriff, right about now I view them as perhaps the only true friends I have in this whole valley."

Walburton looked like he wanted to say more, but could-n't decide what it should be. Finally, he settled for a dis-gruntled sigh before saying, "Very well. Have it your way. I need to go check in on the Widow Clemens...We'll talk again tomorrow."

Chapter 9

"Okay," J.D. said as soon as Walburton and his deputy were gone. "Now that we've done our ducking and dodging for the local law, it's time for some straight talk and straight answers...Belle, we can start with where we had to leave off back at the ranch when you indicated you knew those three men who were chasing your buggy this morning."

"Actually, I only recognized one of them," Belle corrected him. "His name is Hiram Woolsey. He's from San Francisco."

"*Hiram*?" J.D. echoed.

"Describe him," said Kate.

"He's quite tall and thin. Narrow face with heavy brows and a beaklike nose. Long black sideburns. You'd remember if you saw him."

Kate and J.D. exchanged glances. Then, turning back to Belle, Kate said, "That was one of the riders chasing your buggy, alright. The one J.D. and I tipped out of his saddle, the only one we managed to get a very close look at. Unfortunately, he's not one of the ones we blasted down in the barn a little while ago."

"So what was his connection with you back in Frisco?" J.D. asked.

"He works for the Ballard brothers, Frank and Alfred. They own and operate a string of houses...like the one I worked at...in several locations on the coast. He handles problems for them."

"And you rate as a problem?"

"So it would seem. I never understood, until I told them I was leaving the business to get married, how iron-fisted the Ballards were about controlling the girls they had set up in their houses." Belle's gaze shifted somewhat anxiously to Kate. "I realize it's not a very ladylike thing to discuss but, as J.D. said, it's time for straight talk."

"I agree," Kate replied.

Belle nodded. "All right. The fact is, I was quite good at what I did, and very popular. I made the Ballards a lot of money. Which is not to say I didn't get my own reasonable cut in the process. Still, I never saw myself as so damn important to their operation. Hell, they have lots of popular girls. But part of the iron-fisted thing, apparently, is about sending a message. That's the only reason I can think of for them to put so much effort into trying to stop me from leaving before they were the ones to decide they were done with me."

"How did they try to stop you?" asked Kate.

"At first it was just talk. Telling me I was being foolish, that I'd be sorry and would come crawling back. Then there were veiled threats about their 'investment' in me, and how I owed it to them to stay in the game. But it didn't turn seriously threatening until just before Oliver and I were getting ready to leave the city. Hiram and two thugs—neither of the two men who were with him on the trail this morning—accosted us outside our hotel room. Oliver responded to the threats from those original three by striking Hiram and knocking him down. Luckily, Oliver was armed with a pistol at the time, which he drew to back off the other two."

"Good for him," said Kate.

"Too bad he didn't use his pistol to open up on the whole bunch and do for 'em permanent-like," added J.D.

"No one can argue that, not if it would have prevented Oliver from lying over at the undertaker's now, as we sit here talking about it," Belle said glumly.

"So after the trouble in San Francisco," said Kate, "you didn't see or hear any more from this Hiram character until today?"

Belle shook her head. "No. Nothing. Oliver and I thought that whole business was behind us. When those riders showed up this morning, practically right in our back yard, it was a shock."

"How, exactly, did they make their play this morning?"

"Other than the setting, not all that different from the way they threatened us in the city. The one big difference, unfortunately, was that they were prepared for Oliver to be armed. He wasn't wearing a sidearm, though, only a rifle under the seat of the buggy. You see, we were returning from having ridden out to look at the location for the new house Oliver is going...*was* going...to build for just the two of us. With Clay already running most of the day-to-day activity, Oliver wanted us to get away from the current ranch headquarters so we could share our time together more quietly and more privately."

Belle paused for a moment, composing herself, then continued. "At any rate, when Hiram and his men put in their appearance they all were openly and heavily armed and all had their guns drawn by the time we saw them. They came out suddenly from behind some rocks and blocked our way. When Oliver was forced to rein up our team, Hiram and his men crowded in on either side and demanded he throw down any weapons he had. Oliver had little choice but to comply.

"Then they started in with the threats. Hiram did the talking. Told me how much trouble he'd gone to in order to find me. How mad the Ballards were for the humiliation

53

and expense I was causing them, how what I'd done was putting ideas in the heads of some of the other girls and how I needed to be taught a lesson and held up as an example to get rid of those notions in anybody else."

The muscles at the hinges of J.D.'s jaw bunched visibly. "And they aimed to accomplish that by running you over a cliff and killing you?"

Belle shook her head. "I don't think that's what they set out to do. Things got more out of hand than they were ready for. You see, one of the riders—not Hiram—reached out with his knife and cut the reins of our team. Then he claimed he would spook the horses and stampede them into a panic if I didn't cooperate by climbing down and riding away with them. I'm pretty sure it was only supposed to be just another threat, a way of getting me to do what they wanted...

"Only that's when Oliver did something reckless and totally unexpected. *He's* the one who made our horses take off by suddenly whistling and shouting and slapping them across their rumps with his hat. He told me afterwards he thought he could whip the team into breaking away from Hiram and his men and making it onto the range of a neighboring ranch where we'd catch the eye of some friendly wranglers who'd help get the team stopped and, simply by their presence, discourage Hiram's bunch from keeping after us."

"Reckless, like you said. But also gutsy, you got to give him that," J.D. allowed.

The expression on Belle's face showed strains of reliving the experience as she finished relating it. "What Oliver didn't figure, though, was that the team would take out across the hogback like they did, and then stick with it even after the ground turned so rocky and treacherous. By then, it was too late for us to try to jump clear, and the horses were panicked out of control."

"It was a close call, no two ways about it," Kate summed up.

"Too close, and all for so little," Belle added bitterly. "It only bought poor Oliver a few more hours before he fell victim to those same bastards, anyway...All because of me."

"Don't do that to yourself," Kate was quick to say, in a stern tone. "You've been telling us how Oliver loved you and accepted everything about your past. Well, then that meant also accepting the danger associated to it. Neither Hiram nor the Ballard brothers were secrets to him. And as far as danger, he didn't build one of the biggest cattle spreads in this mountain valley without standing up to plenty of risks long before he ever met you."

"Thanks for the encouraging words," Belle replied softly. "And you're right, Oliver faced plenty of risks and dangers building the Bar OB to what it is today. But those kind of things he knew how to deal with. Hiram Woolsey he wasn't so sure about...

"I don't mean he was afraid of him. Not in the normal sense of the word. But the fact Hiram made it clear he was willing to kill me if he had to—rather than let me get away with leaving the Ballards like I did—was a kind of ruthlessness that unnerved Oliver. What was more, exactly because of that, because of the way I was linked to Hiram, we were reluctant to turn to the sheriff for help out of concern that too much of my background would be revealed. In the old days, Oliver would have rounded up some of the men who rode for his brand and they would have gone after Hiram strictly on their own. But some kind of explanation would still have been owed, plus the law would've caught wind sooner or later."

Belle paused, her gaze touching Kate and J.D. each in turn. "Please believe it wasn't the main reason behind inviting you to dinner but, once Oliver had time to consider how the two of you hire out to help folks in trouble and how successful you've been at it, well, he was planning on asking for your help. Naturally, we would have been willing to pay whatever—"

"We don't make a habit of charging money to friends who find themselves in a jam," J.D. said tersely.

"Especially not now that Hiram has made it personal by springing an ambush on us," added Kate. "In fact, you might even go so far as to say you couldn't *stop* us from going after that skunk in order to remove him as any further threat to you...not to mention making him pay for cutting down Oliver."

"The only thing is," said J.D., running a thumb knuckle back and forth across the point of his chin, a habit he had when pondering hard on something, "I ain't all the way sure ol' Hiram or his boys are the ones who shot Oliver."

Nobody said anything for a long minute. The two women sat looking at J.D. like he'd just babbled something in a foreign tongue.

"When Sam Ruckner came here with Belle's note," J.D. explained, "he said Oliver Braedon had been hit by two rifle rounds. You also referred to a rifle, Belle, when you were telling us about the shooting at the ranch. And then the sheriff once again said 'rifleman' just a few minutes ago when he spoke about Oliver getting shot."

"So what of it? What are you getting at?" Kate wanted to know.

"If no one actually saw Oliver get shot, how is it everybody is so convinced he got it with a rifle?" asked J.D.

Belle answered, "While young Jorge was the first one to reach Oliver, there were several other men close enough to have also heard the shots. I think Sam was one of them, as a matter of fact. Anyway, they all agreed it was a rifle. By the sound."

"Okay. That makes sense." J.D. nodded. "To a practiced ear, a rifle shot sounds distinctly different from a pistol."

"Anybody who's been around guns much at all knows that." Kate eyed J.D. "I still don't see the point you're trying to make."

J.D. shrugged. "It's simple enough, really. The men who laid for us—men we know to have been associated with Hiram Woolsey—were all packing handguns only. And when we checked out the two horses left behind by the pair we killed, neither of 'em were fitted with a saddle scabbard. So unless Hiram was the only one who bothered to keep a long gun within reach—which I'd say ain't likely, him coming from a big, crowded city where pistols and in-close belly guns are the more common weapons—I'd be willing to bet there wasn't a rifle in the whole stinkin' bunch."

"So it seems unlikely they'd use a rifle to shoot Oliver and then, only a short time later, show up to try for us with only handguns," said Kate, beginning to catch on.

"Sure makes you wonder," J.D. said.

"And their reason for coming after us at all was simply revenge for us interfering with them out on the trail?"

J.D. nodded. "Trying to get even is a powerful motivator, especially for men who have violent habits to begin with."

"But if not Hiram and his men, then who murdered my husband?" said Belle.

"Finding that out—along with running Hiram to ground for what he *has* done, and keeping you safe in the meantime," J.D. told her, "is the rest of the job we just signed on for."

Chapter 10

The next morning, right after sunup, J.D. rode out to the Bar OB ranch headquarters. Kate stayed behind in Elk City with Belle, to be on hand in case the Braedon offspring showed up before J.D. got back. They were coming to finalize funeral arrangements, that much was already established. But with a night for the fact to sink in that their father was permanently gone now, it wasn't impossible to think that the resentment they felt toward Belle could have taken deeper root, too, and the chips on their collective shoulders might lead to something less subdued and civil than the way they'd behaved when last seen.

As he rode through the crisp early air, putting the lodge and the town behind him as he passed into the flatter, grassier rangeland of the valley, J.D. reflected a bit on what he knew of the history of this place. How a man named Joel Estes, after striking it rich in the California gold fields, had come here with his wife and thirteen children and first saw the potential for raising cattle in the area. A dozen harsh winters, however, was enough to convince Estes that his wealth rated him an easier life so he moved on. But other, heartier souls, like Oliver Braedon, had taken his initial lead and stuck it out to make a go of what had become several thriving herds.

Somewhere along the way, an English duke or earl or some such—J.D. couldn't recall his exact name or title— had attempted to horn in and claim vast sections of the land for his own personal hunting preserve. It didn't take long for the ranchers and a handful of leftover rugged mountain men to send him packing, however. After that, the hunting lodge the Englishman had started to build was completed and expanded into the public lodge where Kate and J.D. were now staying, and soon the town of Elk City was spawned. So, in the end, the whole matter had yielded some positive results.

Nevertheless, looking around him at the mountains and peaks and stands of timber with the wide expanses of grasslands in between, J.D. could only shake his head at the pompous greed of anyone who would think they could ever claim and tame so much raw beauty for their very own. Pieces of it? Maybe. But even then only if and when Mother Nature was feeling charitable enough to go for stretches without reminding puny humans with even the noblest intentions who was the *real* boss of the land.

Moving on from those thoughts, J.D.'s mind next lingered on a bit of more recent, more personal, and far more pleasant history.

In the middle of the night, Kate had awakened him to resume the "honeymoon" friskiness they'd had interrupted earlier in the course of their picnic. One of the best parts of their union was the strong sexual appetite they shared and it had become almost a tradition for them—like a reaffirmation of living as counterpoint to having faced a hail of hot lead meant specifically to end life—that, following their participation in a gunfight, they would engage in a bout of fierce lovemaking.

Nevertheless, J.D.'s first reaction last night had been a momentary reluctance due to concern for the advisability, maybe even propriety, of pursuing such activity with Belle so relatively close beyond their bedroom door, asleep on a day bed in another part of the suite. But his passion for

Kate was never very far from the boiling point so whenever she took on the role of aggressor, her conquest was all but assured right from the get-go. Plus, when it came right down to it, J.D.'s concerns about Belle's nearby presence hadn't really been all *that* great...

"Besides," Kate had whispered feverishly in his ear as her hands were busily, expertly manipulating his rapidly-hardening manhood, "it's not like she's never heard the sound of lovemaking coming from another room before."

It was then that J.D. realized the devilish side to what Kate was up to. Yes, there was their post-gunfight tradition to maintain and Kate's boldness when it came to sex hardly made this the first time she'd been the one to initiate a romp.

But adding spice to this particular occasion—for Kate, J.D. sensed, and maybe even a little for himself, too, if he was honest about it—was the very fact that Belle *was* close by. And if J.D.'s former lover happened to overhear the sounds of their passion, then she could take it as a friendly if non-too-subtle reminder from Kate that *he is mine now.*

Apart from the question of at least partial motive, which really took only a flicker of time in the course of things, the lovemaking Kate and J.D. had subsequently engaged in was intense and wholly satisfying. Seldom had the lush contours of Kate's splendid body felt silkier under his touch or the taste of her sweeter to his probing tongue. Never were her mewlings of pleasure more gratifying to his ear, urging him to thrust deeper and harder and longer until they both exploded in a shattering mutual climax.

Afterward, as they lay sweaty and spent in each other's arms, when he was able to catch his breath again, J.D. had muttered, "Okay. I gotta hand it to you...That wasn't such a bad idea after all."

◆◇◆

In the daylight, the sprawl of the Bar OB ranch head-quarters was even more impressive than what J.D. had been able to discern the night before. Still, amidst the col-lection of outbuildings and corrals and so forth, he had little trouble finding the bunkhouse and adjoining mess hall. Even through the smell of cattle and their inevitable byproduct, the aroma of strong coffee wafting in the air helped to guide him.

Although he well knew that the working day for ranch hands started ungodly early, J.D. was nevertheless hoping he'd find a lingerer or two somewhere around the mess hall. As it turned out, he was right. And, in an even bigger stroke of luck, one of the men he found was none other than the very hombre he was looking for.

When J.D. entered the smoky, low-ceilinged structure through an open doorway, sitting right there at a long, rough-hewn table with a stubby, apron-clad individual whom J.D. took to be the cook, was Sam Ruckner in the act of raising a cup of coffee to his mustache fringed mouth.

"Mornin', Sam," J.D. greeted, flashing an easy grin. "I re-ally hate to interrupt a fella who's concentrating so mightily on hard, gut-bustin' labor, but I wonder if you could spare me a few minutes of your time."

If Ruckner was surprised to see J.D., he didn't let it show. He simply went ahead and finished taking a drink of his coffee.

The cook, on the other hand, got a big kick out of J.D.'s words. He was a moon-faced specimen with shaggy side-burns poking out from under a derby hat and a soggy, half-chewed, unlighted cigar planted in one corner of his mouth. J.D. was willing to bet that the derby, cigar, and apron constituted a uniform of sorts that was as much a part of

61

the man as his skin.

"I don't rightly know who this big fella is," the cook chuckled, "but he's dang sure got you pegged, Sam. He dang sure does."

"Save the commentary, Porkchop," Ruckner grumbled in return. "If you must know, this gent is the famous gunfighter J.D. Blaze...J.D., this overstuffed tablemate of mine is the infamous—leastways that's what he should be, considering how many innocent men he's poisoned over the years with his cooking—Porkchop Myers."

Porkchop tipped the brim of his derby. "Pleased to meet ya. Heard you shot up the town pretty good last night."

"Little matter of self defense. Some misguided jaspers laid an ambush for my wife and me. We had to convince 'em it was a bad idea."

"Yeah, heard that part, too. A gun-totin' female—what'll they think of next?" Porkchop gestured toward the empty bench on the other side of the table from him and Ruckner, adding, "Have a seat, take a load off."

"You up for some of the worst coffee in the world?" Ruckner asked.

As J.D. lowered himself onto the bench, he answered, "Be obliged. Been catching whiffs of it ever since I got onto the property."

Ruckner grunted. "Well, if that wasn't enough to scare you off then maybe you're a brave enough soul to actually survive a cup...Porkchop, get off that lard ass of yours and show our visitor some hospitality."

"He's your visitor, not mine," Porkchop shot back, but he nevertheless rose up and returned in a minute with a steaming cup that he placed in front of J.D. Next to it, he set a plate containing half a dozen biscuits. "Those are left over from breakfast, if you'd care for a couple."

Last night, after things finally settled down, before going

to bed J.D. had raided the lodge's kitchen and from there foraged a roast beef sandwich, a large wedge of tangy cheese, and a bowl of apple slices as means to quell the hunger pangs he was suffering. That had gotten him through the night. But he'd ridden out before breakfast this morning and hadn't been on the trail for very long before his stomach grumbled a stern warning against a repeat performance of attempting to run on empty again for any length of time.

So not only were the biscuits a welcome offer but, when the first bite proved to be fluffy and wonderfully delicious, it was almost too good to be true. Reality hit with a resounding thud only a moment later, however, when a follow-up sip of coffee turned out to be every bit as vile as Ruckner had prophesied. J.D. was thunderstruck by the contrast between the two—how could the same pair of hands that had made such terrific biscuits then produce such awful brew?

Ruckner waited to have a good laugh at the expression on J.D.'s face and then explained the puzzle. "The biscuits got sent down by Maria, the cook at the main house. She made them last night for a certain dinner that never took place, didn't want to see 'em go to waste...The coffee, unfortunately, is strictly the handiwork of Porkchop here."

"Hey," Porkchop protested, "if I had a big, fancy stove and oven and all the hotsy-totsy cooking utensils like Maria does, I could turn out better grub, too. Not that it matters to most of the chow hounds around here. All they need is something to fill their bellies with a lump that'll last to the next meal, and they're satisfied. It ain't like they would appreciate gourmet food if I *did* serve it." He pronounced "gourmet" like "gor-met".

"Well, it's highly doubtful we'll ever know the true answer to that," said Ruckner with a skeptical arch to his brows, "because the day anything close to resembling gourmet food comes off that corncob-burner stove of yours is the day Hell will have frozen over and we'll all be nothing but slabs of ice."

J.D. reached for a second biscuit, deciding this time he'd keep from ruining it by holding off on taking another drink of coffee. "If you fellas ever get tired of slingin' insults back and forth," he said around a mouthful of fluffy goodness, "I'd still like to squeeze in a couple minutes of your time, Sam."

"Sure, sure, J.D.," Ruckner said. "I was allowed to bunk in a little extra this morning because I didn't get back until late after driving Mrs. Braedon and the boss's body into town. The bad thing about that, though, is that I woke up to no company except this damned old bacon burner and his usual cantankerous attitude. Be glad as hell for somebody else to talk to."

"I'll remember that," Porkchop responded. "Next time you ain't here when grub is served and you still want something to eat when you *do* show up, I'll remind you that meals are served at certain times and then I'll leave you go hungry."

"No, you won't," said Ruckner, rising to his feet. "Because that would be too much like doing me a favor and you wouldn't be able to live with yourself if your sorry ass ever did that for anybody."

Porkchop's round face took on an expression somewhere between a scowl and a look of bemusement. "You might have a point there...Damn, I hate it when you're right."

"Come on, J.D., let's talk outside," Ruckner said, motioning. "Grab yourself another couple of those biscuits if you want."

♦◊♦

"So you're sure it was rifle shots you heard?"

"No doubt about it," Ruckner answered.

"And right around here is where the boy saw the haze of gunsmoke hanging in the air?"

"Uh-huh."

J.D. and Ruckner were standing on the back side of a small corral located near the north edge of the ranch head-quarters layout. A carriage barn was about a hundred yards off to their left and sixty or so yards to their right was the main house. Behind them, the cleared land abruptly ended and fell off in a rock-strewn slope choked with un-derbrush and stunted trees. At the bottom of the slope, a shallow gully or dry wash twisted away crookedly in either direction.

"Did the sheriff or anybody examine this area very closely after the shooting?" J.D. asked.

Ruckner shook his head. "Not to speak of. I mean, those of us who came running at the sound of the shots were more interested in looking after Boss Braedon. I guess a couple of the fellas came over this way to make sure the shooter still wasn't lurking around, but that was about it."

"Nobody heard the sound of a horse riding off or any-thing?"

"Nope. Had that been the case, you can bet some of us would have been tearing after it."

J.D. got down on one knee and ran his fingers through the grass. "The sheriff told Mrs. Braedon the angle of the bullets that hit Oliver matched with coming from over here. So he must have poked around a little."

"Yeah, I guess I did hear something about that," Ruckner allowed. "I was heading out to bring that note to you and your wife about the time the sheriff showed up, so I can't say for sure what all he done. But it was getting onto dark by then, so conditions for seeing to poke around wouldn't have been the best."

"Which may be why," J.D. said, plucking a small shiny object out of the grass, "he didn't spot this."

Ruckner leaned in and scowled at the spent shell casing that J.D. held up. ".40 caliber. From a Henry repeater," he declared.

"Uh-huh," J.D. agreed.

"So it was a rifle that was shot from here, just like everybody's been saying. Don't see where that gains you anything."

J.D. grinned. "Verification. Satisfaction, my friend." He dropped the shell casing in his shirt pocket, then asked, "I suppose there's no shortage of Henry repeaters amongst the ranch hands hereabouts?"

"Not so's you could notice. Most of the boys will pack a long gun, in case of running into bigger varmints, when they ride out into the brush. Some favor a Winchester, some a Henry. Probably 'bout an equal mix."

While J.D. was digesting this, movement over by the house caught the eye of each man. They turned their heads to watch a woman emerge from the rear of the house carrying a basket of laundry. By her copper skin and long, flowing black hair, J.D. judged her to be of either Spanish or Indian blood. She was no longer young but her bold-featured, unlined face made her exact age hard to judge—it could have been thirty, it could have been forty. The long skirt and off-the-shoulders peasant blouse she wore showed a somewhat thickened waist yet a form that was still attractively curvaceous, made especially so by a pair of proudly thrusting breasts. When she bent over to set the basket down, the front of her blouse sagged open to reveal a very generous amount of cleavage.

"Quite a handsome woman," J.D. muttered.

"You ain't wrong there, son," agreed Ruckner. "But you

should have seen her twenty-some years ago when she first came to this valley. One look at her sucked every ounce of breath out of your body and made you want to drop to your knees right on the spot and give thanks to the Man Up-stairs for creating something so fine, even if all you *ever* got to do was only look."

J.D. cut him a sidelong glance. "And for all these years that's all you've ever done...just look?"

Ruckner sighed. "Afraid so. You see, Maria came here—Maria, that's her name, by the way—as the bride of my friend Alfredo Sandimez. 'Fredo, Porkchop, and me were the first wranglers to hire on for the Bar OB. 'Fredo became the first ramrod for the outfit. Until he got killed in that damn freak horse fall. By then, him and Maria had a son. Any-way, after 'Fredo was gone, it fell to the rest of us to sort of look out for Maria and the boy, Jorge. Before long, Boss Braedon took her on as a housekeeper and cook to help Dorothy, the first Mrs. Braedon, who was in frail health and always suffering from one ailment or other. With Dorothy's ailments and four young kids to raise up and all, having Maria on board worked out good for everybody.

"In the last few years before Dorothy passed, even though the kids were fairly grown by then, Dorothy kept getting sicker and sicker. So Maria stayed on. And then even after Dorothy was gone. Her and Jorge have become sort of fix-tures around here, almost like part of the family, I guess you could say."

"Almost, but not quite," J.D. amended. "And all the while you've pined over her, but never made your move."

Ruckner shrugged again. "Reckon that's the size of it. The time just never seemed right...Plus, I never could shake the feeling that, even though he was dead, I'd somehow be betrayin' my old pal 'Fredo."

After setting down her basket, Maria had paused to regard the two men who were watching her. Somewhat abruptly, without hanging any of the clothes on the line that was stretched between two tall posts, she turned away and went back into the house.

"Guess she's kinda shy," J.D. observed.

"Yeah, she's like that."

"I suppose us standing here gawping like a couple of rutting coyotes wasn't smart, either. Probably be enough to unnerve any woman." J.D. jerked a thumb over his shoulder. "Come on. I want to have a look down in that gully, see if I can spot any sign of where a horse might have been tied or passed in and out of there recently. Then I'll get out of your hair and leave you to your work."

"Okay. But, before you light out, I want to hear some first-hand details on that horse barn shootout. The sheriff and his deputy clamped themselves around you so tight last night that I couldn't get close enough to talk to you at all."

Chapter 11

When J.D. and Ruckner came back up out of the gully, having found nothing of any significance, their attention was quickly drawn by new activity taking place in the back yard of the big house. This time four people, none of them Maria, appeared there. They immediately began heading at a brisk pace toward the small corral behind which J.D. and Ruckner now once again stood.

"Uh-oh," J.D. muttered. "That don't exactly look like a welcoming committee."

"I've seen friendlier faces on a pack of pissed-off Arapahoes," agreed Ruckner.

Clay Braedon led the quartet, wearing a scowl that would have been the envy of even shaggy-browed Sheriff Walburton. His sister and two brothers marched behind him, each of them displaying their own fierce glower, like it was a contest for family honors or something.

J.D. and Ruckner came around the corner of the corral to meet them.

"You again," sneered Clay when he and his siblings had drawn to within a few yards. "What the hell do you think you're doing snooping around on private property?"

"Doing no harm that I know of," J.D. answered. "Just looking over the site of the ambush."

"Way I heard it, you had your own ambush in town last night. Why don't you stick to nosing around there, instead of showing up here where you haven't been invited?"

"I got the okay from your stepmother."

"My *stepmother*!" Clay spat out the word like it tasted bad in his mouth. Then his eyes jumped to Ruckner. "I see you're Johnny-on-the-spot when it comes to being mixed up with this interloper again. Don't you have ranch chores you're supposed to be doing?"

Ruckner's expression stayed flat. "You gave me leave to lag a bit this morning on account of getting back from town so late last night. Remember?"

"Lagging 'a bit' don't mean lagging half the goddamn day," Clay snarled. "Nor is it any kind of allowance for escorting around this—"

"Best you yank your spurs back outta the meat, mister," J.D. cut him off. "If you got a beef with me, keep it between us. This man did nothing but show me a little friendly accommodation when I looked him up to ask a few questions."

It was then that Chuck, the second oldest Braedon son, decided to join in. He stepped aggressively forward, standing shoulder to shoulder with Clay. He was leaner, slightly taller, but clearly stamped from the same mold, with the familiar pale yellow hair, lantern jaw, and ruddy complexion. He was reportedly the most hot-headed of the bunch and J.D. had no trouble believing that, the way his eyes flashed with intense anger.

"Who the hell do you think you are, coming 'round here telling us how to act and how to treat our hired help?" Chuck demanded.

This, in turn, got an unexpected rise out of Ruckner. "'Hired help'?" he echoed. "Why, you young pup, I was working this land and wrangling the cattle on it when you was barely off your ma's tit and still leaving piss puddles in your pants. In all that time I was never called or treated like just one of the 'hired help'. Your dad was alive to hear you spout off like that, he'd knock you flat on your ass."

"Yeah, well the old man *ain't* alive. Not no more," Chuck sneered. "And that's just the start of the changes around here, some of 'em way overdue."

"That's just plain disrespectful...to Father *and* Mr. Ruckner," spoke up Curtis, the youngest son.

Chuck kept his eyes on Ruckner, and kept the sneer on his face. "In order to be *dis*-respectful, you got to have had some respect in the first place. And that ain't never been the case for me, not when it comes to this old slacker."

"That's enough," barked Clay. "This ain't the time to get into any of that. I'll remind you, Chuck, that I ramrod the crew and if I need any help handling the men, I'll ask for it. In the meantime, keep your opinions to yourself." His eyes cut to Ruckner. "And if I were you, Sam, I'd get in the habit real quick of showing better judgment when it comes to who you side with around here."

Ruckner narrow-eyed him. "What's that supposed to mean?"

"You figure it out. But do it on your own time. You've had enough of a lag on your morning start, I'd suggest you go find something useful to do."

Ruckner hesitated, glancing uneasily at J.D.

"Go ahead, Sam," J.D. told him. "I'm done here anyway."

"That tears it!" Chuck exploded. His eyes whipped wildly from Clay to J.D. to Ruckner, then back to Clay again. "You gonna just stand there and watch that old mossback take his orders from this so-called gunfighter, this slick who's obviously honeyed up to dear old Step Ma, angling to siphon off some of the Braedon money she figures to inherit?"

"That's a lie," J.D. said. His voice was low, but the ice in his tone froze everybody to silence.

Nobody spoke. Nobody moved.

Finally, Chuck gulped a ragged breath and then swallowed. The sound of his throat muscles working and his Adam's apple sliding up and down seemed unnaturally loud.

"Nobody calls me a liar," he said, barely above a whisper.

"I just did," J.D. stated calmly. "If you didn't hear it plain enough, I'll be glad to say it again."

For the first time, Nora Braedon spoke. "This is ridiculous. We've heard all about you, Mr. Blaze. Goading Chuck into a gunfight would be just another form of murder. Don't you think we've already suffered enough of that? For God's sake, our father isn't even in the ground yet."

J.D. kept his focus on Chuck. He'd already made his assessment of Nora. Seventeen, good figure, the family blonde hair. Same strong lines to her facial features but softened by femininity just enough to make her rather pretty in a bold, not dainty, kind of way.

"You got no call to beg for me, Sis," Chuck said. "I ain't exactly a stranger to handling a gun, you know. This conniving meddler don't scare me. Just because he has a big reputation don't mean nothing. Hell, half of the gunnies like him roaming the West made their reputations as back shooters or from outdrawing drunks who couldn't hit their mouth with the next drink, let alone fumble out a pistol."

J.D. smiled thinly. "You keep telling yourself that, son. When you get to Hell, you can swap stories with the other sorry jackasses I sent there who felt the same way."

Suddenly, Clay Braedon twisted sharply to his right, the side Chuck was on, slashing up and around with his elbow, driving it hard against the side of Chuck's jaw. The younger brother staggered back, his knees starting to buckle. Clay turned the rest of the way and lunged after him before he went all the way down. He grabbed him by the shirtfront with one hand, cocked the other fist and drilled a punch to the point of his brother's chin, knocking him cold.

"Clay! What are you doing?" Nora cried out.

She and Curtis rushed to seize Chuck by the shoulders and ease him to the ground after Clay let go of him.

Clay wheeled back to face J.D. He was breathing hard and his fists were still balled. His eyes fell to J.D.'s drawn Colt, which had blurred from holster to fist the very instant Clay had started to raise his elbow.

"You still itching to shoot him, even now that he's unconscious?" Clay said.

J.D. studied the man's face. There were many emotions darting in and out of the expression there. Clay was scared, scared for his younger brother's life. And he was angry—angry about the murder of his father; angry at the hot-headed foolishness of his brother; angry at J.D.'s presence. But most of all, in his eyes he was pleading, without saying it in so many words, for J.D. to show some mercy.

J.D. spun his Colt then re-holstered it. "I can wait. I figure he'll sooner or later give me cause all over again, after he wakes up."

"You *wanted* him to draw on you. You prodded him into it. And if he'd tried, you wouldn't have hesitated to shoot—maybe kill—him."

"I disagree. I neither wanted what was about to happen nor prodded him into anything he wasn't already primed for. But when a man insults me, I call him on it. If it leads to slapping leather, a person in my position can't afford to take that lightly. So you're right on one thing...I wouldn't have hesitated to do what I had to."

Clay continued to regard him. "Last night you were invited to dine at my father's table. When he first mentioned it to me, I thought a measure of friendship was implied. Now I can only wonder what your true motive was."

"Yesterday at this time," J.D. said, "my only motive to be in this valley at all was for enjoying a stay—along with my wife—at the Big Thompson Lodge. We decided we'd earned a little rest and relaxation after wrapping up a particularly tough job down near Denver. Taking the honeymoon we never had, she liked to call it...But the events of last night have changed things. Now it ain't about being here to relax no more. We aim to stick around and help get to the bottom of who killed your father. At the same time, we mean to make sure nothing happens to your stepmother."

"Last night she introduced you as an old friend."

"That's true."

"So seeing to her best interests trumps everything. Is that it?"

J.D. scowled. "*Protecting* her trumps everything. Way I see it, doing that and finding out who killed your father are two ends of the same rope."

"Maybe, maybe not. In case you haven't figured it out, the four of us" —Clay made a gesture to include himself and his siblings— "don't necessarily harbor such warm, nurturing feelings toward Belle."

J.D.'s eyes took on a trace of flintiness. "Uh-huh. All the more reason she needs somebody around with a different outlook."

From where he lay on the ground, head resting in his sister's lap, Chuck stirred faintly and emitted a pained groan. Nora lifted her face and glared at her oldest brother. "Damn you, Clay. I think you broke his jaw!"

"I highly doubt it. His skull and everything attached is too damn thick to break that easy," Clay responded. "But, even if you're right, he's better off alive with a busted jaw than he would have been if I hadn't stopped him from doing something that was sure to get him killed."

Cutting his eyes back to J.D., Clay said, "All the same, I expect he'll be a whole lot easier to keep tamed down if his eyes don't fall on you the first thing he comes around. Plus,

I think you and me have said about all there is to say to one another. At least for the time being"

J.D. returned the man's gaze for several beats. At the same time, he could feel the heat of Nora's glare having shifted to him. The youngest brother, Curtis, merely seemed to hover on the periphery of things, uncertain what to say or do.

Finally, J.D. nodded. "All right. I'll be on my way then." He turned his attention to Sam, who also had been standing quietly by ever since Chuck's angry outburst that nearly ended in gunsmoke. "See you around, Sam."

"Yeah, reckon you will. I'll be ridin' out with you, if you don't mind," Sam came back.

Clay's face clouded. "What's that? What do you mean?"

"You heard me plain enough. Just like I heard that young pup plain enough a couple minute ago." Ruckner stabbed a finger in the direction of the still-sprawled Chuck. "Lot of changes coming around here now that Boss Braedon is gone. Don't expect none of 'em are gonna favor me, or that I'm gonna like 'em much in return. So I figure it's time for me to dump the coffee grounds, kick out the fire, and move on."

"I'd expect you to keep a cooler head, Sam. Act a little more sensibly," said Clay.

Ruckner cocked his head to one side and gazed back stubbornly. "A body expects a lot of things in life. Sometimes you flat get disappointed...I'll be taking my good saddle, my two ponies, and whatever personal belongings I got in the bunkhouse with me when I leave. I'll be around town for a while. You can figure up what I'm owed in wages and send it in with one of the boys next time one of 'em heads that way."

Chapter 12

It took next to no time for Ruckner to get his things in order. He said his goodbyes to Porkchop but no one else. Looking on, J.D. could see signs of regret and sadness in the parting of the two old pards. Shortly after that, with Ruckner leading his spare horse, they were putting the Bar OB ranch headquarters in the dust behind them.

The size of the sparse bundle that constituted the total of Ruckner's personal belongings, tied now on the back of his second horse, struck a chord in J.D. A man's whole life summed up in two nags and a bundle of items that included little more than a battered envelope of personal papers and photographs, a winter coat, a new pair of boots not yet broken in, and a handful of clean clothes—most of them worn and washed, some already with patches.

J.D. wondered how many other wranglers and drifters scattered across the West could claim little more, maybe not even as much. Hell, up until he'd met and married Kate, he hadn't fallen very far out of that category himself. Yeah, he'd made good money selling his gun all over Hell's creation. But then he'd spent it damn near as fast...Until Kate came along and set him to thinking about planning for the future; to a time when they could eventually quit doing gun work and roaming from job to job, instead settling down comfortably together in a spot where they could spend whatever time they had left just enjoying their memories and each other.

J.D. shook off these ruminations and brought his mind back to the present. That "settled down" time was still a long ways off, especially now that he and Kate found themselves unexpectedly plunked down in the middle of this situation full of bitter feelings and an ambusher (or ambushers, plural) who had already killed once and—judging from the attempt in the lodge horse barn—was ready and willing to strike again.

In his own mind, J.D. was convinced that, whoever shot and killed Oliver Braedon, it was *not* Hiram Woolsey or either of the two gunnies who were part of the attack on the Blazes. That didn't rule out the possibility Hiram might have hired a fourth shooter, a rifleman, to do the job on Braedon...but J.D. wasn't ready to buy that, either. Not for a minute.

No, he felt sure there was some whole other angle—or motive, as Clay Braedon would put it—behind the Braedon murder. The fact it came at a time when Hiram Woolsey happened to also have shown up in the valley, seeking to settle an old score with Belle, was only a misleading coincidence.

J.D. had plenty of opportunity to mull these things over as he and Ruckner rode along. The old wrangler was understandably in his own reflective mood, leaving neither man much inclined toward making small talk.

After they'd covered about half the distance to Elk City, though, an exchange of words became warranted.

"Something wrong?" J.D. asked when Ruckner reined his mount down from the easy canter they'd been maintaining.

Ruckner pointed off to the north, the direction his head was turned. "Up there. That twist of smoke...it don't belong."

J.D.'s eyes tracked to where Ruckner was pointing. Just short of a mile away, rising up from a tree-smothered ridge of higher ground, a curl of grayish smoke was spiraling skyward.

"That's still Bar OB land, lessen I'm off on my calcu- latin'," Ruckner continued. "No call for any of our riders— which means nobody with a legitimate reason—to be up that way. Especially not stopping to build a fire."

"The overnight camp of a drifter passing through?" J.D. suggested.

"Possible," Ruckner allowed. "But somebody just passin' through would more likely stick down lower, where the passage is flatter and emptier. All rugged ground up there, and choked with lots of trees. Why pick the most difficult route available?"

J.D. set his jaw. "If not somebody passing through, then maybe somebody with cause to find an out-of-the-way spot to lay low, do a little wound-licking and re-grouping."

"Whoever it is, for whatever reason," Ruckner said, "can't help thinking it seems a mite strange."

J.D.'s mind raced. Once back in town, he'd been figuring to go in search of trying to pick up some kind of lead on the elusive Hiram Woolsey. Hit the saloons, hotels, boarding houses and so forth, do some asking around, some arm- twisting if he had to. Elk City wasn't especially big as far as its permanent population, but it got a lot of folks passing through, some staying on a temporary basis—prospectors, miners, and cow punchers looking for work, as well as those who came for the hunting, fishing, or just plain sight- seeing to be found in the surrounding mountains and lakes.

Those who could afford it stayed at the lodge and utilized the services of the old mountain men who lingered in the area to hire out as guides. The rest, those less flush or some who considered themselves savvy enough to venture out on their own, either pitched outlying camps or stayed at one of the town's cheaper establishments for their time in the vicinity.

J.D. had reckoned Hiram, due to his big city background, as somebody who'd choose the latter. Now, however, having been foiled twice and with his accomplices blasted out of the picture, could it be he'd feel desperate enough to retreat to the wilderness in order to avoid exactly the kind of thorough, in-town search J.D. had in mind?

Once the thought cropped up, there was no way to ride on without checking it out.

"A-course," said Ruckner, scratching vigorously under his whisker-stubbled chin, "since I no longer ride for the Bar OB brand, it ain't no skin off my nose, not no how."

J.D. cut him a sharp sidelong glance. "Cut the bullshit. You know you still care and you also damn well know what I'm thinking."

Ruckner sighed. "Yeah, I expect I do. You got more of a one-track mind than a man with his britches on fire headed for the nearest watering trough."

"So," said J.D., eyeing him, "you know the best way for us to maneuver up close to that smoke with the least chance of being seen?"

"Son," Ruckner answered loftily, "I first set foot on this land when there was Arapaho everywhere, thicker than fleas on a buffalo herd. Notice I still got my hair? Way I kept it was from knowing the terrain like the back of my hand and because not even a beetle bug skittering between blades of grass can get around quieter and sneakier than I can...Follow me."

♦◊♦

Little more than half an hour later, J.D. and Ruckner were picking their way quietly, cautiously through underbrush and trees as they eased up on the campsite from which a curl of smoke was still rising.

Ruckner had first led the way down into a shallow draw and then angled over to a tree-lined creek in order to take them out of sight from anyone who might have been watching from the high camp. It would have looked like they were merely leading their mounts to water. Once obscured from sight, however, the pair had stayed under the cover of tree foliage. Cutting back, they ascended quickly until they reached a point where they had to abandon their horses and cover the rest of the distance on foot.

Reaching the perimeter of the small natural clearing where the campsite was set up, the men spread a dozen yards apart and closed in like the points of a pincer. Scanning the scene, still from concealment, it appeared the camp was abandoned. The fire had died down to a pile of smoldering ashes and charred chunks of wood still issuing a skyward-crawling trail of smoke. What looked like the wadded up blanket from a bedroll and a few cooking utensils lay bunched together on the far edge of the clearing, but there was no sign of current human activity.

J.D. felt a clutch in his stomach that he first took for frustration at coming up empty. But then, as he continued to hold and study for an extra measure, he decided it was more a feeling of uneasiness about something. Before he could signal Ruckner to stay put for a minute longer, the old wrangler rose up out of the bushes and strode out into the clearing, cursing loudly.

"What kind of damned fool rides off and leaves his fire burning? It ain't all that dry yet, being only early summer, but it still would take just a single spark to set—"

The gunshots blasting out of the underbrush on the back side of the clearing cut short his words and the slugs punching into him sent Ruckner jerking and twisting sharply under the impacts. He pitched onto his right side, hitting the ground hard, crying out in pain and surprise as he went down.

While Ruckner was still falling, J.D.'s Colt leaped into his fist and he instantly began returning fire, aiming at the cloud of gunsmoke marking where the shots had come from. His teeth clenched, bared in an angry grimace, J.D. fanned the Colt's hammer and sent six rapid-fire rounds sizzling across the breadth of the clearing.

The second the last chamber emptied, J.D. shifted from his own position—ducking low to the left, hitting and rolling smoothly, coming up closer to where Ruckner had fallen. Even while his body was still in motion, his hands flew to the urgent, swift, well practiced activity of immediately reloading his gun. It seemed almost impossible to think he hadn't scored some kind of hit with his volley of return fire, but there was no way to be certain. Plus, there was the remote possibility that Hiram Woolsey—if that's who it was over there—might not be alone. He might have already hired some replacements for the two comrades he'd lost the previous night.

As he was snapping shut the Colt's loading gate, J.D. got at least a partial answer in the form of three more shots sailing across the camp and shredding the underbrush back near where he'd initially been. To J.D.'s trained ear, the shots sounded like they matched the first two that had taken down Sam, meaning they came from the same gun. The good news about that was that it indicated only one shooter; the bad news was that it indicated J.D. hadn't scored a serious enough hit to put the gunman out of commission. J.D. swore under his breath. On the assumption it *was* Hiram he was dealing with—and J.D.'s gut instinct insisted that had to be the case—the Frisco thug was one lucky S.O.B.

Just for the hell of it and just to give the ol' Hiram something more to think about, J.D. snapped off a couple loosely aimed shots and then shifted his position again. He was closer to where Ruckner lay now. He couldn't get a good look at the old wrangler through the thick brush he was forced to remain behind, but he thought he could hear the wounded man breathing raggedly. J.D. knew he couldn't allow this cat-and-mouse shootout to drag on for very long or Sam's chances of staying alive would slip drastically. What was more, if the ambusher was ruthless enough and noticed his victim still breathing, he might spend a couple additional slugs to finish the job.

"When are you gonna be ready to start acting like a man, you ambushing coward?" J.D. called out. "Is that the only way they know how to do things in the big, bad city of San Francisco—sneak attacks and back shootings?...How about the two of us step out there in the open and settle this the rest of the way, face to face? Just to show there's no hard feelings, I promise to haul your carcass on down to Elk City and see to it you get a decent burial...after I blast what passes for guts out of you and send your black soul to burn in Hell!"

J.D. waited.

But there was no reply. Only silence...except for the ragged, gargling intakes and exhalations of breath coming from Ruckner's still form.

J.D. began moving once more, sticking to the concealment of the underbrush, this time edging silently and steadily around the perimeter of the camp clearing. If he couldn't shame Hiram into showing himself, he'd have to try and force him out, flush him like a jackrabbit.

He'd only circled about half the way to where he estimated Hiram to be when J.D. heard the slap and snap of somebody moving hurriedly and carelessly through the brush. It sounded like his quarry was making a run for it. But J.D. had to stay cautious; it might only be some kind of trick. He continued edging along, listening intently. Then, from somewhere in the distance, he heard the snort and whinny of a horse followed quickly by the sound of retreating hoofbeats.

J.D. cursed. With a sinking feeling, he knew the elusive damned Hiram Woolsey had given him the slip yet again.

Chapter 13

"You know," said Doc Beedle, wiping his hands on a bloodstained towel as he emerged from the treatment room at the rear of his office, where he had been tending to Sam Ruckner behind the closed door, "the undertaker, Corradine, made me an interesting offer this morning. He wanted to bet me to see which of us would tally the most customers during the time you two are in town."

With the latter, his weary, seen-it-all eyes settled on J.D. and Kate, who'd been seated in the outer office waiting area but had risen to their feet when the doctor appeared. "Naturally," the doc went on, "I turned him down, thinking he had me at a distinct disadvantage. With this latest development, however, maybe I should reconsider. If we take into account those who are merely in the *vicinity* of your...er, activities, then perhaps I'd have a chance at beating that old ghoul after all."

J.D. met Beedle's gaze with a scowl. "So, in your long-winded way, are you saying Ruckner is going to pull through okay?"

"Yes, he is."

"Thank God!" breathed Belle Braedon, who stood with Kate and J.D.

"He'll never have full use of his left arm again," Beedle added. "The bones in his shoulder are busted to hell and gone, nothing I could do but stop the bleeding, clean out as many fragments as possible, and then brace his arm so the knitting can start. Once it sets, I expect his hand and arm below the elbow will function okay. But, above the elbow, it'll basically be locked in place. After that, how he handles this limitation mentally will be the thing to watch."

"I thought he was shot twice," said Kate.

Beedle nodded. "The other slug hit under his arm. Went in at the outer edge of his armpit, exited at an angle out through his pectoral muscle. I cleaned it good, left it to mend itself. It'll be stiff and sore as the dickens for a while, but should have no lasting effect."

Also present in the outer office area, standing by quietly, were Sheriff Walburton and his deputy, Walt Early.

Walburton stepped forward, cleared his throat. "Now that you got assurance Ruckner is going to make it okay, what are your intentions, Blaze? You figure to go after the one who did it?"

"*We* figure to go after him," Kate answered.

"And that's for damn sure," J.D. confirmed.

"You realize, of course, there are legally appointed individuals for that kind of thing, and laws to be followed to see that justice gets meted out properly."

"You saying you intend to go after that bushwhackin' bastard yourself?" J.D. wanted to know. "If so, you ought to already be on the trail."

"Maybe he means he wants to deputize us," Kate suggested.

The sheriff went tight around the mouth. "I don't appreciate being made sport of, ma'am."

"Then don't leave yourself open for it," Kate told him.

"So what's your point?" J.D. prodded the lawman. "You don't mean to try and stand in our way, do you?"

As if with regret, Walburton shook his head. "I got no legal basis for that. You're free to come and go as you please. But if you keep shooting people and stirring up trouble in my territory...Well, you may force my hand."

"What do you expect them to do?" Belle demanded stridently. "Wait around for another ambush attempt. And another after that—until *they're* the ones riddled with bullets?"

Walburton held up his hands, palms out. "Calm down, Mrs. Braedon."

"I *won't* calm down! How can I be calm with people getting shot and dying all around me?" Sparks danced in Belle's eyes. "What's more, if that remark about 'stirring up trouble' was meant to include me and the issues that arose this morning between myself and Oliver's children, you can go to hell. And if you or anybody else thinks I'm going to allow myself to be pushed around by that pack of spoiled brats just because they were born with the name Braedon— a name that only carries any significance due to the hard work and sacrifice of their father—then you've all got another think coming!"

What Belle was referring to was an incident that had occurred while J.D. was away from town for the extended amount of time it took to go explore the suspicious smoke, get bushwhacked, then tend to Sam as best he could at the scene before building a travois to transport the wounded man slowly, carefully down off the rugged high ground and eventually on into town.

While all of that was taking place, Clay and his siblings had shown up to meet with Belle and the preacher to make final arrangements for Oliver Braedon. That went okay and was over quickly. But Clay and the others weren't done. They had some further business that involved a lawyer they brought with them.

The shyster presented Belle with papers that comprised a hardline threat to block the revised will Oliver had drawn up providing for Belle to have the new house, the ten acres of land, and the percentage of earnings from all Bar OB business. Boiled down, what the legal mumbo jumbo contained in the paperwork amounted to was a claim that the revised will was "predicated" on the new house having been built and occupied by Mr. and Mrs. Braedon for a period of time before the occurrence of Oliver's demise. Inasmuch as none of this had happened yet—the building of the new house not even *begun*, as a matter of fact—it was the shyster's contention that the new will was not yet in effect and therefore the will as it stood prior to said revisions should be the binding document.

Of course Belle had the right to hire her own lawyer and contest this interpretation through lengthy court proceedings. Or, it was subtly suggested, perhaps a monetary settlement could be agreed to that would save everybody concerned a lot of time and trouble and public airing of grievances.

This piece of nastiness had just been laid out and both Belle and Kate—who'd been on hand throughout (yet, to J.D.'s amazement, hadn't once drawn her gun and threatened to shoot anybody)—were freshly seething when J.D. rode in dragging Ruckner behind.

The legal shenanigans were put on hold, naturally, in view of the news of yet another ambush and the dire condition in which Ruckner was delivered. It was only in the doctor's waiting room, while the medic was intently at work behind the closed door, that J.D. was brought up to speed about what Clay and the others had sprung. By then, the whole bunch had left town and headed back to Bar OB ranch headquarters, not even bothering to check on the status of the old wrangler who'd been there with their father at the start of the spread.

"Really, Mrs. Braedon. Let's be fair," Sheriff Walburton said now, in response to Belle's angry outburst. "I had no hand in the family dispute that arose earlier. And I assure you I have no side in the matter. My only role is to encourage everybody to keep a cool head and make sure individual behavior stays within the limits of the law."

Belle's nose crinkled up like she'd caught a bad smell. "Oh sure. Now tell me how that buddy-buddy Wednesday night poker game you sit in on every week with Clay and Chuck and their pipsqueak of a lawyer won't make any difference on the way you look at things. Just like the fact your deputy has been sniffing around Nora Braedon like a dog in heat for the past six months won't have any influence his outlook...

"In case you haven't figured it out by now, Sheriff, I'm not some shy, oh-gosh little farm wife. I know when the chips are stacked against me and I know when the house has its thumb on the roulette wheel. But none of that will stop me from digging in and making a fight of it, even if all I ever accomplish is breaking off that thumb and ramming it up somebody's—"

"Belle!" J.D. cut her off. He aimed a disarming grin. "You'd better calm down before you blow a gasket. And, in the process, you might want to work on remembering that you're a lady."

"I think she was doing just fine," Kate remarked. "That 'lady' stuff is overrated, if you ask me."

The sheriff, face red-mottled, cleared his throat again. "Seems like a good time to remember what I said a minute ago about everybody keeping a cool head. To help that along for right now, probably the best thing is for me and Walt to take our leave."

J.D. nodded. "No argument. But here's something else to remember: With Kate and me gone on the trail of the bushwhacker who shot Sam, Belle will be left alone here in town. I guess you already know she's making arrangements for her own suite at the lodge, since it's been made clear she is no longer welcome out at the ranch. Given all the tension in the air and the question of whether or not Oliver Braedon's killer might be somebody other than this jasper we're going after, I think some concern for her safety is warranted. I want your assurance you'll see to that while we're away."

"I can take care of myself, J.D.," Belle insisted.

J.D. ignored her. His eyes stayed on Walburton. "I'll hold you personally responsible if any harm comes to her."

Deputy Early took a step forward, with his hackles up. "That sounded dangerously like a threat, mister."

J.D. snorted dismissively. "Call it a threat, call it a promise, call it whatever you want, sonny. Just remember it. Do that, there'll be no need for me to follow up on what I said."

Walburton put a hand on his deputy's shoulder, turned him toward the door, pushed him firmly in that direction. Neither looking back nor saying anything further, the two lawmen left.

"Not that I'd be up for gunplay or anything like that," Doc Beedle said after they'd gone out the door, "but, if it will help ease anyone's mind, I can make it a point to look in on Mrs. Braedon now and again. From what I overheard, I don't hold at all with the high-handed tactics being employed by Oliver's children. Not at all."

"You needn't go to the extra bother, Doc. I'll be fine. Really," Belle told him.

"Or," Beedle said, his wispy white eyebrows raising, "there may be another alternative. When my patient in the next room comes out from under the anesthetic and is ready to be moved, he'll need somewhere to stay. If I know hickory tough Sam Ruckner like I think I do, even weakened from blood loss and with only one arm, he could still mount considerable resistance in the face of any trouble. What if he came to stay with you, Mrs. Braedon, while your other guardians are away? It might cause a few tongues to wag, but the two of you could look after one another and I'd have all the more reason to drop in from time to time to check on the both of you."

Belle's eyes gleamed and her mouth curved upward in an impish grin. "What a splendid idea! When I get back to my suite, I'll arrange for an extra bed to be set up. And if Sam staying in my quarters scandalizes some of the old biddies in this town, well, getting the dust shaken off their bustles would probably do them some good."

J.D. and Kate exchanged glances.

"Sounds like a plan," said Kate.

J.D. spread his hands. "Works for me."

Chapter 14

It was the middle of the afternoon by the time J.D. and Kate left Elk City. They rode straight and hard for the abandoned campsite where Ruckner had been shot.

"Because Sam was bleeding so bad and needed all my attention," J.D. related once they arrived at the clearing and had dismounted for a follow-up examination of the scene, "I couldn't afford much looking around at the time. While I was hacking down some saplings and twigs for the travois, though, I took a quick peek over there, where the shooting came from. Direction I heard the horse take out of, too."

He and Kate walked over to where J.D. had gestured. "The ground drops off, as you can see, and it looks like there's a little creek down there. My guess is that Hiram—since I'm convinced it's him we're talking about—was down there watering his horse, probably filling his canteen, getting ready to head out. That's likely why he hadn't yet killed his fire all the way and still had the blanket and part of his mess kit to pick up. I figure he was coming back up the slope to finish striking the camp when he spotted Sam entering the clearing, cussing about the still-smoldering fire...A minute later, *Hiram* would've been the one here in the middle of the clearing and we could have gotten the drop on him."

"If wishes were fishes..." Kate muttered, peering down the slope, through the trees and rocks, to where a narrow, twisting stream glittered in the dappled light.

91

"Yeah. Ain't that the truth." J.D. sighed. "Well, let's go ahead and lead our horses on down. Nothing more to see here. If we're gonna pick up that skunk's trail, down there's where we'll find it."

As they turned back to where they'd ground-reined their mounts, the sounds of somebody else approaching the clearing reached them. It clearly wasn't anyone attempting stealth, so there seemed to be no reason for alarm. Nevertheless, strictly out of habit, the Blazes spread wider apart from one another as they slipped the keeper thongs off the hammers of their pistols and then let their hands hang loose and ready near the grips of the weapons.

The sounds drew closer until three horsemen emerged from the brush at nearly the same point J.D. and Kate had entered the clearing only a few minutes ago. The impression given was that the three had followed a similar path of ascent to reach this spot.

The middle rider was Chuck Braedon. The other two were nondescript wranglers J.D. couldn't remember having seen before.

Chuck's expression was no friendlier than the last time he'd faced J.D. The only difference was some noticeable swelling and a hint of bruising on the side of his face where his older brother's elbow had struck earlier that morning.

Without preamble, Chuck said, "You're trespassing on Braedon land. And you ain't welcome here."

"Don't you get sick of spouting the same line?" J.D. said tightly. "I know I'm getting pretty sick of hearing it."

"You don't like it, quit coming around. Pretty simple solution. What's more, I really don't give two squirts of green apple shit what you're sick of."

"Appreciate it," J.D. responded, "if you'd watch your language around my wife."

Chuck sneered. "Yeah, I can see she's a real delicate

flower. Packing iron just like the 'slinger all those stories claim her to be. You expect me to believe she's gunned down anywhere near the number of men she's supposed to have, yet I have to be careful of not saying a couple cuss words in front of her?"

"No, I don't expect you to believe it," Kate spoke up. "You know why? Because you look too mule stubborn and stupid to take a piece of friendly advice, that's why."

"You're right about one thing," said Chuck, both his tone and expression hardening. "I'm plenty damn stubborn. That's the real reason I'm here. I heard you two were planning to go after whoever it was shot old Sam. That's why I've been on the lookout, figuring you'd try to pick up sign where the shooting took place. Me and him"—he jabbed a finger to indicate J.D.—"have got a piece of business to finish, and I'm stubborn enough to want to get it done."

"Best be careful what you wish for, Chuck," advised J.D. "Your big brother ain't around this time to save you from getting serious hurt."

"Yeah. That's the whole idea."

Chuck swung down from his saddle. The other two men stayed where they were.

"How many kinds of fool are you?" Kate said. "You ever stop to think that the man we're going after might be the same one who killed your father? And by interfering with us—out of pride or stubbornness or whatever you're calling it—you're also interfering with us catching up with him?"

"I figure the law will take care of running down my pa's killer. If they don't, me and my brothers will see to it ourselves." Chuck wagged his head. "None of that matters to what's about to happen here."

He stepped around in front of his horse and planted his feet wide. His curled hand hovered over the six-shooter holstered on his right hip. Over his shoulder he said to the wranglers still in their saddles, "You know your role in this. I'm out for a fair fight. You two get involved only if the woman tries to join in. She does, go ahead and cut her down."

"We've already lost too much time getting started on what we came here for," said J.D. He settled into his own stance. "Ain't got none extra to waste on a jackass like you...Whenever you're ready to die, Chuck, go ahead and make your play."

For the first time, a flicker of uncertainty showed in Chuck's eyes. But it was gone as quick as it had appeared and then all that was left was his determination to go through with what he'd set in motion.

The blinding-fast draw that came next, however, was from the hand of neither Chuck nor J.D.—it was Kate's Colt leaping into action. Three times the gun spoke, the shots crowded so close together it sounded like a single echoing report. All three slugs tore into the holster and gun on Chuck's right hip, ripping apart leather, spanging off the cylinder and handle of the Remington that had been secured there, jarring it loose.

The ruptured holster coughed out the gun like a sick dog upchucking a piece of bad meat. The Remington hit the dirt. Chuck staggered a half step backward, twisting slightly at the waist, reaching with both hands to clutch his hip where the destroyed holster had hung. He dropped to one knee.

Kate lifted her Colt higher, sweeping it in an arc that covered the two stunned wranglers still on their horses, then bringing it back down to where it was loosely aimed at Chuck once again. "I got three shots left, one for each of you," she announced. "I pull this trigger again, it will be with intent to kill."

Chuck lifted a hand from his hip and the palm was

smeared with blood from where a bullet had ricocheted off the Remington and plowed into meat and bone. "I'm hit, boys," he wailed. "That bitch shot me!"

J.D. took a step toward him. "I warned you about swearing in front of my wife—that damn sure includes swearing *at* her." He swung his leg in an upward arc and drove the toe of his boot to the point of Chuck's chin. Spewing a minigeyser of bloody spit, Chuck flopped back and down, landing heavily on his shoulders and then sprawling there, motionless.

Now J.D. spun to face Kate. "What the hell do you think you're doing?" he demanded. "That was my play all the way!"

"Tut-tut," cautioned Kate. "Now you're the one swearing at me."

"Because you deserve it! What right did you have to horn in?"

Before answering him, Kate wagged her Colt at the two wranglers. "Shuck your guns," she ordered them. "Then climb down and go stand over by your boss. Stand real still until I say otherwise."

The men complied, sullen-faced but without comment.

"I'm waiting for an answer," J.D. said to Kate, showing some sullenness of his own. "You had no call to get involved."

"Yes I did," Kate replied calmly. "If I hadn't, you would have killed him."

"Just as sure as the rising and setting of the sun. I left him alive the last time, and look where it got me." J.D. scowled. "Come to think on it, we're starting to make a dangerous habit of leaving too damn many people alive in our wake. We left those three jaspers alive on the ridge yesterday morning, and what did that lead to? It got us bushwhacked and then Sam ended up nearly paying with his life."

Kate's lush mouth pressed into a tight, thin line. "Okay. Maybe you're right about that part," she allowed. "But that still wouldn't have made killing this fool a smart idea. No matter what else he is, he packs the name Braedon and there's no denying that name carries a lot of weight in this valley. If you'd gunned him—fair fight or not—you know damn well that would have made things sticky for us."

"We've been there before...and still did what we needed to."

"Sure. That's fine for us. But what about Belle?" Kate's eyes searched J.D.'s face. "You and I can always ride away. Blast our way out if need be. Only Belle don't have that option. Everybody will continue seeing her as linked to us, to what we do. I don't know if she plans on staying around here or not. But whether she does or doesn't...does she need the added grief of what you gunning Chuck would heap on her?"

J.D. tried to hold Kate's eyes. But couldn't. He looked away, instead fixing a glare on where Chuck lay, still unmoving. "You two," he growled at the wranglers standing on either side of the fallen man. "Get him on his feet and then on his horse. Then the lot of you beat it the hell out of here. When he comes around, tell him that if I see him coming at me again, I'll just flat open up on him. No questions, no talk. No nothing but I put him down permanent-like."

"What about our guns?" one of the wranglers asked uneasily.

"Leave 'em. You can come back for them tomorrow...Now make dust, before I change my mind."

Chapter 15

J.D. and Kate had no trouble picking up Hiram's trail on the creek bank down at the bottom of the drop-off. It led off to the north and for the most part remained easy to follow inasmuch as it stuck closely to the meanderings of the creek. In a handful of instances, where the rippling water cut a narrow passage through upthrusts of jagged rock, the tracks would swing out wide to one side or the other, only to converge again when the creek's path ran through easier terrain.

After three hours of this, with the long shadows of evening thickening fast as the sun began to sink behind the higher peaks of the Rockies, the trackers decided on a likely spot to pitch night camp.

"You figure he's headed for some particular place," Kate asked as they stripped down and picketed their horses, "or just fleeing blindly?"

"At first I thought that—that he was just bent on getting clear of where he shot Sam and away from me in case I'd given chase right away. But after this far, he should have figured out I wasn't on his heels. That being the case, I'm surprised he hasn't swung out to more open country, where he could travel easier and faster." J.D. wagged his head. "I'm beginning to reckon now that he *is* headed for a particular place."

"Where would that be? His familiarity with the area has to be pretty limited. How could he know a place to aim for?"

97

"He's been around long enough to hear talk," J.D. pointed out. "It could have even come from those two he had riding with him—we don't know where he took them on."

"You mean he may have hired them from around here?"

"Not impossible, I'd say." J.D. made a sweeping gesture with one hand. "There's mining camps all through here, all along the front range. You know what you find in mining camps...In addition to the hard-working miners, you find the dregs who flock in to try and take advantage, looking to make easy money off their back-breaking work. Gamblers, prostitutes, con artists, pick pockets and petty thieves, flim-flammers of every stripe."

Kate nodded. "Even some who'd hire out for gun work. I see what you're driving at."

"The nearest mining camp I know of to the north—the way Hiram is headed—is Silver Dog. Been around a while, ought to have considerable size to it by now." J.D. shrugged. "I ain't saying that's where Hiram hired those first two rowdies. Hell, I got no way of knowing that. But it don't really matter. Silver Dog is still a place he could have heard about. And he'd fit right in there, whether he's looking to just lay low for a while or wanting to hire some more guns to back him up."

"I guess his trail will tell the story when we pick it up again in the morning," allowed Kate. "But you've got me convinced where it probably is going to lead us. How far is this Silver Dog?"

"Only a handful of miles, if I got my bearings right. We should be there easy by noon tomorrow."

"And then what?" Kate said. "I mean, exactly what is our intent if and when we do catch up Hiram?"

"Why, we're going to stop him from going around shooting at people—namely us and those around us."

"By killing him, you're saying."

"Surest way I know of. It's what he's been asking for."

"But what about the question of whether or not he was responsible for ambushing Oliver Braedon? We kill Hiram, we'll never get the answer to that—not out of him. And we've already done for those two who were riding with him."

J.D. scowled. "Damn, girl. Don't you ever run out of questions?"

"I'm just saying there's more than tracking down and killing to take into consideration here," Kate said stubbornly. Then her own fine features darkened with a scowl. "And here's another...If we leave Hiram alive to say whether or not he killed Oliver, then that means he'll also be alive to blab about why he's in these parts to begin with. In other words, he'll reveal Belle's past in San Francisco."

J.D. looked at her. "For somebody who, in the beginning, despised Belle for being a floozy I had a tumble or two with in the past and then somebody who'd likely only married Oliver for his wealth, you're sure showing a lot of concern for her well being."

"In case you never heard, bub," Kate responded, "it's a woman's prerogative to change her mind. Besides, I already explained how I'm a sucker for an underdog who keeps showing spunk, even when the odds are stacked higher and higher against them. You saw how Belle barked back at the sheriff and his deputy. I wish you could have also seen how she tore into those Braedon brats and their slick-tongued lawyer when they all thought she was only going to cower and cave in to whatever they wanted...No matter what she might have been in the past, there's a lot to admire about the gal Belle is now. And I mean for us to help her through to the best results possible."

Neither of them said anything more for a minute or two.

At length, J.D. puffed out his cheeks and then released a gust of breath. "All right. You've given us plenty to keep in mind. Part of it, though, is going to come down to what kind of hand we get dealt when we catch up with Hiram. If possible, we need to try and get out of him whether or not he had a hand in shooting Oliver. But we can't take it past a sensible point of risk. He may give us no choice but to kill him...Or, if he's good enough, he may get lucky with his next ambush and take it all out of our hands, permanent-like."

Once the horses were taken care of, they set to preparing the campsite for their own needs. A fire was soon crackling, with a pot of coffee brewing over it and strips of bacon sizzling in a frying pan. While Kate was busy with the meal, J.D. spread out their bedrolls and stocked in more wood to keep the fire stoked through the coming colder hours of the night.

As full darkness settled in, they sat close together by the fire, enjoying cups of rich, strong coffee and eating the bacon along with some delicious biscuits Kate had coaxed out of the kitchen staff at the lodge. After the discussion on a final confrontation with Hiram, conversion had been sparse, each of the Blazes lost in their own tense thoughts. Now, however, with food and drink warming their stomachs and drowsiness after a long, eventful day starting to overtake them, their moods once more began to relax.

"I've got to hand it to you, J.D.," Kate said around a bite of biscuit. "You really know how to put together a relaxing vacation. We've got an already paid-for luxury suite sitting empty back at the finest lodge in the territory, and here we are getting ready to spend our night on the hard, cold ground in the middle of the mountain wilderness."

"Yeah, but look at those stars starting to shine through up there," J.D. said, gazing skyward. "By midnight, up here in this clear, thin air, they'll look so bright and shiny and close it will seem like you can reach out and touch 'em...You can't find that in no lodge suite, not even the finest one anywhere."

Kate gazed at him instead of the sky. "Will you pluck one down for me, J.D.?"

He turned his head to meet her eyes. "I sure would if I could, darlin'. I wish I could pluck great big handfuls of 'em and sprinkle them over you like the for-real diamonds you deserve."

Kate smiled a smile even more dazzling than diamonds *or* the stars. "What do I need with a bunch of clinking, rattling ol' diamonds? I've already got everything I want...you."

Their heads tipped together. What started as a tender, affectionate kiss soon intensified into something more.

Something much more.

They set aside their coffee cups and scooted back away from the fire, their lips parting only briefly and only as much as absolutely necessary. When they reached where J.D. had spread the bedrolls, side-by-side, they lay back, embracing.

"You are a shameless hussy," J.D. murmured against Kate's hungry lips and probing tongue as she unwrapped one of her arms from around him and unerringly moved her hand elsewhere. The fingers slipped under the waistband of his pants in front and began doing some probing of their own.

"If that was supposed to be a protest, it sounded like a mighty weak one," Kate murmured in return. "What's more, a certain part of you"—inside his pants, her hand closed around the throbbing shaft of his rock hard manhood—"seems not to be protesting at all."

"You can't pay no attention to that ol' rascal down there," J.D. told her. "You know he's never shown much in the way of good sense."

"You'd better get settled on the notion that I intend to pay a great deal of attention to 'that ol' rascal down there'. For what I want from him, good sense isn't required. Instinct will do just fine...and, if memory serves, his instincts in that department have proven just fine in the past."

As their kisses grew more heated, J.D. shifted his own hands down between their bodies in order to unbutton his pants. When he'd opened the trousers sufficiently to give Kate's busy hand more room, she began pumping him in long, increasingly insistent strokes. J.D. moved his hands back up, as far as Kate's breasts. He cupped the firm globes, thumbing their nipples through the thin fabric of her blouse and the chemise worn underneath. Kate groaned, nipples hardening immediately.

When J.D. stopped fondling her breasts and started to unbutton her blouse, Kate pushed herself to a sitting position and then lifted her hand out of his pants to nudge away his fumbling fingers. "Let me do that," she said breathlessly. "You get your own clothes off. Hurry! Baby, I want you so bad I can't wait."

First their gun belts were hurriedly, awkwardly unbuckled and set aside. Then, in no time at all, Kate's blouse and waist-length chemise were removed. As was J.D.'s shirt. Each of the lovers displayed splendid physical conditioning. J.D. was all hard muscle, with a curly pelt of chest hair and a flat, ridged stomach. Kate was a wondrous landscape of creamy skin rising and falling in a flow of delicious hills and valleys. Her smooth, flawless skin seemed to glow silver in the moonlight. And her generous, uptilted breasts swelled proud and inviting, capped by pinkish-brown tips that jutted out, begging—no, *demanding*—to be kissed and tongued...which J.D. wasted no time doing, with starving, aggressive abandon.

"Oh, God! You're driving me crazy," Kate gasped.

Frantically, they began baring themselves below the

waist. Both left their boots on. J.D. merely shoved down his already-unbuttoned trousers. His fully engorged member sprang free like a predator ready to strike. Because she was wearing a split riding skirt that could not be simply lifted, as a more conventional skirt or dress might have been, Kate also shoved her lower garment down, revealing a tuft of pubic hair a little darker than the lustrous blond spill that swirled about her head and face.

While his mouth clamped over one of her breasts, J.D.'s hand dove between Kate's legs. His thick middle finger found her already moist and ready as he probed with vigorous expertise.

Kate arched her back in ecstasy. "Sweet Jesus, lover man...That feels wonderful, but you know what I want down in there instead. Don't keep me waiting any longer!"

Seconds later, they were coupling with the practiced movement and rhythm of lovers who are very familiar with one another. Slowly at first, with low murmurings of affection. Then gradually faster and harder. Then at a slower pace once more, but only briefly. Finally, they built to a pounding, passionate frenzy that climaxed in an intense mutual release that left both of them gasping and sweating and spent.

"See?" said J.D. afterwards, when he could catch his breath again. "Who needs a luxury lodge suite when we've got the luxury of each other?"

"Maybe," Kate allowed. Then, her eyes twinkling in the flicker of campfire light, she added impishly, "But what if I need a little more convincing before the night is over?"

"I'll do my best," J.D. replied with exaggerated seriousness. "But you know how that ol' rascal down there has a mind of his own...I don't know if I can hold him back from doing just a *little* more convincing."

Chapter 16

"Am I the only one feeling a cold spot between my shoulder blades, like somebody has a gun muzzle pressed there?" Kate asked, somewhat casually, as she and J.D. steered their horses down the main street of Silver Dog.

"No, there's enough of that feeling to go around," J.D. assured her. "I just wish it *was* a gun barrel jammed in my back—that'd mean some sumbitch was standing close enough to where I'd at least have the chance of grabbing hold of him. This way, the only chance is that any window or doorway might suddenly have a bullet sizzling out of it."

"Then remind me again, why are we putting on this brash display right out in the open?"

"Because I'm sick and tired of playing cat-and-mouse with that damned Hiram," said J.D. "I mean to flush him out. The quicker the better, so we can go ahead and get done with him once and for all."

Kate said, "You realize, of course, that even though his trail led here, Hiram may have only swung this way in order to stock up on supplies. Possibly stay the night. He could already be on the move again."

"Anything's possible," J.D. allowed. "But he can't afford to keep running forever, not if it means coming up short on the job he was sent to do and reporting back empty-handed as far as having dealt with Belle. The way she described those Ballard brothers, they wouldn't react kindly to failure like that, and Hiram ought to know it better than anybody...No, I think it's way more likely ol' Hiram came here looking to hire himself some new gunnies to back his play. And then it'd just be a matter of time before he heads back to Elk City with his aim set on Belle again. What we need to do is stop him short, right here in Silver Dog."

Kate pursed her lips. "Okay. Sounds like you've chewed the matter mighty fine."

"Yeah," J.D. sighed, one side of his mouth lifting in a lop-sided grin. "I had plenty of time to give it a good thinking-over while I lay nice and quiet and peaceful in my bedroll last night."

"Uh-huh," Kate replied, keeping her lush lips pursed and adding a mildly arched brow to her expression. "I had a nice restful night, too, in that fresh, clean mountain air. For a while, though, some kind of little twig or something kept poking at me before I was finally able to roll out of the way and get good and comfortable."

They plodded on silently for a ways after that, each displaying smug, satisfied smiles over the tension-breaking banter and the teasing digs they'd gotten in on one another.

At two hours short of noon, Silver Dog was every bit as busy and boisterous as you would expect for a rugged mining camp. Actually, its size and sprawl was enough for it to be considered a full-fledged town. But most of its inhabitants probably weren't interested in that distinction. A mayor, a town council, a constable...those type of civic embellishments hardly fit the concerns of the rough-and-tumble crowd who only cared that they had a place—no matter what you called it—to buy goods and services that included the availability of plenty of whiskey and fleshly delights.

And, judging from the numerous gaudy establishments mixed in with the other businesses lining the main drag, none of that appeared in short supply.

At the far end of the street from where they'd ridden in, J.D. and Kate found a livery stable that looked both sizable and well kept. A flat wooden sign nailed high between two posts read simply: LIVERY. And below that, in smaller letters: *Hank Brimbel, prop.*

As soon as J.D. and Kate reined up before the sign, a slat thin woman wearing a shapeless felt hat, a flannel shirt, and baggy bib overalls tucked into high, thick-soled work boots emerged from the open double doors of the low-peaked barn. She had a three-tined pitchfork in her right hand and, in her left, clenched a big blue hanky that she was using to mop sweat on the sides of her neck. The wild profusion of gray-streaked, damp-tipped reddish curls that tumbled free from the confines of the hat framed a narrow, plain-featured face and a toothy, friendly smile.

"Mornin', folks. You just arrivin' in town?" she asked.

J.D. nodded. "That we are."

"Welcome to you, then. My name's Hank Brimbel. That's 'Hank' as in short for Henrietta, by the way. But the Hank on the sign there, that ain't me. That was for my husband. His name was Henry but everybody called him Hank, too. We was Hank and Hank." The woman emitted a kind of honking laugh. "Folks really got a kick out of that."

"I bet they did," J.D. muttered.

"What about your husband?" Kate asked. "Did he...?"

"Yeah, the old fool up and died on me," Hank said. "Worked himself to death. Left all this—and the work that goes with it, mind you—to me. Some might see it as he wanted me to work myself to death, too. But I don't buy that. He was too kind a soul for that. Besides, if that was his intent, it didn't work very well. He's been gone nigh two years now, and I'm still kicking."

Kate smiled. "Indeed you are."

"But enough of that. I tend to prattle on sometimes,"

Hank declared. "You folks plan on being with us for a spell? Or just a short stay?"

"Remains to be seen," J.D. said somewhat tersely.

"Most likely not for very long, though," Kate added in a friendlier tone. "But, either way, we're looking to have our horses tended to and put up for a while. If you've got room."

"I got plenty of room, miss. My rates are fair, and so is my care." Hank flashed another wide smile. "I'm thinkin' about adding that to my sign one of these days—you know, like what they call an advertising slogan."

"It's clever and catchy," Kate allowed. "You should go ahead and put it on there."

"You got a lot of competition in town that you need to advertise against?" said J.D.

"Not really. The Buford House, that big hotel 'bout halfway back down the street" —Hank gestured with the hand still clutching the big blue hanky— "they got a kind of corral set up out back where they board a few horses for some of their guests. But that's about it." She brought the hanky back to the side of face and patted at some more sweat. She momentarily patted away her smile, too. "Fact is, some folks don't cotton much to doin' business with a female."

"The real fact," Kate said, scowling, "is that some folks are too rude and stupid to be let loose in public."

Hank shrugged. "Luckily, there ain't too many of that kind around. I get by okay."

"How about horses to sell?" J.D. said, changing the subject. "You got any nags on hand that are for sale?"

"Reckon I do. But," Hank added, her smile returning, "since you put me in the role of a seller, guess I ought to object to callin' 'em 'nags'. What I got is strictly fine horseflesh."

"I'm thinking we might want to add a pack horse when we ride on from here," J.D. explained. "What I'd want would be something good and sturdy but still capable of moving at a pretty good clip if need be."

"I got a few I think would fit that description. Why don't you climb on down from those saddles. I'll lead your horses on back and start getting 'em stripped down while you look over the animals I got for sale."

It was while they were following Hank through the livery barn that J.D. spotted what the ruse about possibly wanting to buy another horse was really meant to accomplish. In one of the side stalls, there was a black and white pinto gelding exactly like the one Hiram Woolsey had been riding the first time they'd encountered him up on the hogback ridge, when he and his two accomplices had been hoorahing the Braedon buggy. J.D. and Kate exchanged quick sidelong glances and Kate gave a barely perceptible tip of her chin to indicate she was seeing the same thing.

It wasn't like there was only one pinto in all of the Rockies' front range, of course. But they weren't all *that* numerous, and the markings on this one fit damn near perfectly to J.D.'s memory of the animal he'd tipped Hiram off of.

"Hold it a minute," J.D. said, halting Hank.

When Hank looked back questioningly, J.D. jabbed a thumb to indicate the pinto. "This horse here," he said. "You been boarding him long?"

Hank shook her head. "Uh-uh. He ain't one of the ones I got for sale."

"I understand that. Thing is, he looks mighty familiar to me. About six months back, see, there was a fella who rode with us for a while. We ended up parting ways, for reasons that don't matter. But danged if this horse sure don't look like the one he was riding back then." J.D. glanced over at Kate. "Don't you agree?"

"Yeah. Looks the same to me," Kate said.

"Reckon it might be, then," Hank allowed.

"Well, if it is, if our old riding pard is in town, we wouldn't mind looking him up and having a chin wag with him," J.D. explained. "His name is Woolsey, by the way. Tall, thin fella with dark hair and long sideburns."

Hank looked thoughtful. For the first time, her appraisal of the Blazes—in particular the way they wore their guns and carried themselves, not to mention the fact that Kate happened to be a gun-packing, beautiful woman—was evident. She gave the impression, J.D. decided, of being someone who didn't miss much but at the same time was careful of showing just how much she took in.

"Description sounds about right," Hank said after a pause. "Can't say about the name, though. He didn't leave one. Showed up late last evenin', was tuckered out and in a hurry to get himself situated somewhere for the night. Paid in advance to put up his horse for two nights and two days. Said he'd be back around if his time in town stretched out any longer."

"And you ain't seen him since?"

"Nope."

"Don't suppose you happened to notice which way he headed after he left off his horse?"

Hank shook her head. "I got busy with the animal. He just headed up the street. That time of night there was still a couple eatin' places open, plenty of saloons and the like where...well, if what they got to offer was what he was lookin' for."

"If I know Woolsey," J.D. remarked, "one of the saloons'd be where he headed first...Anyway, if he should come around again before we run into him, tell him J.D. and Kate are in town looking for him. Will you do that?"

"I will for a fact."

◆◇◆

Forty-five minutes later, J.D. and Kate were seated at a checkered cloth-covered table near the rear wall of a narrow, high-ceilinged restaurant called Stroheim's. The interim, since leaving the livery stable, had been filled by taking a leisurely stroll up and down the boardwalks lining either side of Silver Dog's main street. The primary purpose for this was to get themselves seen, make their presence in town known, and—by the display of guns around their waists and the Winchester Yellowboy J.D. carried slung over one shoulder—leave a clear impression what their stock in trade was.

In the course of the stroll, they had paused frequently to gaze at shop window displays, greeted other pedestrians with nods and friendly smiles, and slowed their steps to glance covertly through batwing doors into the smoky interiors of each saloon they passed. At one point they'd stopped at the mouth of an alley to watch two young black boys do acrobatic stunts and perform energetic dance routines to the talented banjo strumming of their legless father.

"You ever catch me making noises like I'm feeling sorry for myself about something," J.D. muttered to Kate as they walked away, after dropping a generous donation into the hat that rested upside down on the ground beside the banjo player's stumps, "I want you to take the butt end of this rifle and clop me alongside the head just as hard as you can."

During their walk, from one end of the street to the other, the delicious aromas wafting from Stroheim's had been beckoning J.D. Finally, with the noon hour nearly at hand, he could resist no longer and so had steered their course inside.

"It beats me," Kate marveled, "how you can worry so

much about eating at a time like this, when the turn of every corner holds the potential for somebody waiting to jump out and pump your belly full of lead instead of food."

"A body needs nourishment all the same. If for no other reason than to keep up the strength for shooting back," J.D. replied. "It's as simple as that."

"For you, maybe."

"So you're not going to eat anything, then?"

Kate looked aghast. "Are you kidding? You think I'm going to sit here and watch you stuff your face while being bombarded by all these wonderful smells and not have something for myself? A gal's got to keep her strength up too, you know."

Their order was taken by a stout, rosy-cheeked woman with a thick German accent and iron gray hair worn in a severe bun. She returned first with tall steins of dark beer, followed shortly by platters of schnitzel and fresh-baked rye bread along with bowls of sauerkraut and hot German potato salad.

Despite the fare proving every bit as excellent as its aroma had promised, both of the Blazes nevertheless exercised the discipline to keep from stuffing themselves too full. This was naturally more difficult for J.D. than Kate. But for anyone who made his or her living with a gun, it was nearly as important to avoid getting bogged down by a heavy meal as it was to keep from impairing one's reflexes with an excess of alcohol.

As Kate and J.D. enjoyed their meal, the remainder of the restaurant filled to capacity with a hungry, boisterous lunch crowd. The eating establishment was clearly and deservedly very popular.

From the vantage point of the rear table they had chosen for that very purpose, J.D. and Kate carefully scanned the faces of all who entered. None seemed to warrant closer scrutiny...None, that was, until the profusion of gray-streaked curls framing the unsmiling countenance of Hank Brimbel came into view. They watched as she threaded her way the length of the place and came to a halt in front of their table.

"I see you found your way to the best vittles in town," she said above the din of conversation and the clank of plates and pans.

J.D. nodded. "If there was any better, I'd surely be surprised to hear it...Would you like to join us? There's plenty of room at the table, we could grab an extra chair from somewhere."

"No, but thanks for the invite all the same. I've got to get back to my business." Hank's eyes narrowed with a mixture of curiosity and concern. "You happen to run into the fella you was askin' about earlier—that former runnin' pard of yours?"

"Not yet," Kate answered somewhat guardedly, trying to read Hank's tone and expression.

"Didn't think so. But it so happens he's also lookin' for you two. In a way, you might even say he found you. Leastways, he knows where you're at...That's why I'm here. He sent me."

"Sent you to do what?" J.D. wanted to know.

"To tell you where you can find him. Where he's waitin' for you."

J.D. set his jaw hard. "Where?"

Hank leaned closer. "Far end of the street, to the north. Down in the flat near the creek. Where the burned-out shell of the old Buford House hotel stands—the original one that got wiped out by fire when the town was first starting up."

"He give a name?" Kate said.

"Said you'd know who he was."

"He alone?"

112

"Didn't see anybody else. But I don't know that I'd put a whole lot of stock in that."

J.D. slid his chair back from the table. "You got any kind of law around here?"

Hank shook her head. "Not really. Got what they call a Miners Council that tries to handle claim disputes and such. Half the time nobody pays attention to their rulings, though. Things usually come down to who shoots the fastest and surest and is the one still standing when the argufyin' is over."

"Good. Just the way I like it," said J.D. "How about an undertaker? Town got one of them?"

Hank nodded.

"Good again. Somebody might want to suggest for him to get a pine box or two nailed together."

Hank placed her hands flat on the table and leaned her face in closer to J.D. and Kate. "Okay. It's clear what you're fixing to go do. Just like it was clear what you came here for, and that this ain't your first trip around the dance floor together. But hear me good: This hombre who sent me here...he's pure snake mean and dangerous. I could see it in his eyes and smell it oozing off of him."

"What do you see when you look in our eyes?" Kate asked.

"I see danger there, too...But what I'm afraid I don't see is the snake meanness you're gonna need to match."

Chapter 17

"You don't believe that Hiram is waiting for us alone, do you?" Kate asked.

J.D. gave a single shake of his head. "Like Hank said, I wouldn't put a whole lot of stock in it. Not for a second. If Hiram didn't have somebody new hired to back him up, instead of inviting us to a face-to-face he'd be running like a cat slapped in the ass by a boot jack."

"So we're walking into another ambush. A trap."

"No, we're walking toward what Hiram *means* to be a trap. If we don't let ourselves get caught in it, it just might snap shut and backfire on him."

They were once again walking down the main drag of Silver Dog, having reached the north end where the boardwalks and buildings tapered off and stopped. The street became a winding, deeply-rutted road that eventually disappeared over a long hill and meandered off to the outlying digs and whatever lay beyond. Twenty or so yards ahead and to their right, as if the rest of the town had purposely separated itself from the bad luck spot, they could see the charred timbers and mostly collapsed ruins of what Hank had identified as the original Buford House hotel. It lay downslope from the road, in the center of what had once been a broad clearing now choked with weeds and sapling growth. Farther down was a staggered line of ash, cottonwood, and fir trees that marked the path of the same nameless creek they had followed from the ambush campsite.

J.D. stopped walking and gave the scene a final close

scrutiny. "What I'm thinking," he said, "is that I'll angle down from here and walk out in the flat area between the ruins and the creek. If Hiram is going to stick with the pretense of a straight-up confrontation, that's a likely spot to start it off."

"What about me?" Kate asked.

"How about you go on ahead a ways further, then start making your way down along the far side of those ruins?" J.D. pointed. "If Hiram's got backup bushwhackers waiting like we figure he does, some of them are sure to be waiting in there. Maybe all of them, but I got a hunch there'll be some in that tree line down by the creek, too."

"If that's the set-up, you'll be walking into a crossfire."

J.D. shook his head. "No, not with you for the boys in the ruins to contend with. They're bound to see you coming so they'll have to worry about you before they do me. All you've got to do is keep from getting picked off before you've spotted your targets for when the blasting starts."

"When will that be?"

"Since it seems like Hiram wants to make a show out of it this time before we get to the actual shooting, I figure he'll have his boys on hold until he opens the ball himself. Should give you plenty of time to get in a good position."

Kate's brows furrowed with concern. "But you'll be out in the open pretty much all the way. When I get down in amongst those ruins, I may not be able to keep you in sight for at least part of the time. And if you're right about Hiram having men over in that tree line, too, then you'll still have lead coming at you from two directions once things pop— from the trees and from Hiram."

"There's plenty of scrub brush and young trees down there for me to squirm in behind. I'll make out okay. You just worry about keeping your own pretty self out of the way of any flying lead and do what you have to in amongst those charred timbers. If we're going to try and take Hiram alive and allow him to duck for cover, those ruins will be the closest place for him...You may end up with him smack in your lap."

♦◊♦

After exchanging a quick kiss for luck, they parted and started on their separate courses.

In addition to the Colt riding on her hip, Kate was also armed with a .44 caliber Starr Army Model revolver, with a six inch barrel, tucked in the waistband of her split riding skirt at the small of her back. J.D. was packing his own Colt and once again wielding the Winchester Yellowboy. If this combined firepower wasn't enough to get the job done against Hiram and his hired coyotes, then there was little chance they'd be in a condition to fire any more rounds, anyway.

J.D. started down the slope.

The sun was hot on the back of his neck. Internally, though, a kind of cool, calming current was running all through him, mind and body alike. His hands were steady, his ceaselessly sweeping eyes were clear and alert. This was what he did. What he was good at—one of the best around.

His gaze flicked momentarily in the direction of Kate. The same, he knew, was true for her. The Ice Princess, when it came to gun work. In the beginning, when they'd first started riding together, there had been a time or two when the concerns and protective inclination any man would naturally feel toward the woman he loved had caused J.D. to partly lose focus—due to worrying about Kate—on his own part of the action they were involved in. This lack of concentration slowed him enough so that it only added to the risk of the situation for both of them. After that, and after getting roundly chewed out by Kate, he'd learned to put his fears and concerns aside and have complete faith in her coolness and competence.

His angular approach brought J.D. even with the creek end of the burnt rubble, what he assumed had once been the front entrance to the hotel. Another quick glance showed that Kate was no longer in sight, having been lost behind the sloping ground, scrub brush, and sapling growth. J.D. strode out into the open area in front of the ruins.

Up closer now and down on the flat, he saw that the remains of the old hotel were more substantial than he'd first realized. Long stretches of the stone foundation, though blurred by weed growth, were still standing, as well as a handful of blackened wall sections and a few thick, half-charred beams leaning at odd angles here and there. Two towering stone chimneys, rising up from what J.D. judged had once been great hearths at either end of the structure, stood mostly intact. The one back toward the slope was partly fallen away but the nearest one stood tall and square-topped even though the hearth around its base was only rubble.

More places in there to hide than he'd figured, J.D. thought somewhat sourly as he took a stance before the ruins. As if on cue, reminding him that there also were other places for concealment to stay aware of, a low breeze moaned from the direction of the creekside line of trees.

Squaring his shoulders, lifting his chin, J.D. called out. "Woolsey! Hiram Woolsey!"

His voice hung hollow in the emptiness for a long moment.

And then Hiram appeared, emerging from the shadows underneath a scorched timber tipped against a corner of stone foundation. He came forward until he was standing in the sunlight a dozen feet from J.D.

He was medium height, lean and narrow-faced, with dark eyes under a ledge of black brows and thick sideburns flaring flamboyantly wide at the corners of his jaw. He was clad in striped pants tucked into high boots and a gray coat flared wide open to reveal a black-handled pistol thrust into a wide blue sash worn around his waist.

Hiram licked his lips and then spoke in a moderately high-pitched voice with a heavy nasal twang. "You've been wanting a face-to-face meeting. Well, here we are."

J.D. kept his own voice and expression flat, unreadable. "Uh-huh. Just the two of us, is that it?"

Hiram's top lip curled into a sneer. "You think I don't know about your pretty blond partner sneaking down the slope over my shoulder?"

"And I'm supposed to not figure you've got men hidden all around the edges of our little confab here? Bushwhacking is a hard habit to break, from what I understand."

"'Bushwhacking'." Hiram snorted. "What a ridiculous term. One I was blissfully unfamiliar with back in the city, back in civilization where I come from."

"What did you call it? 'Backshooting'? Or just plain old 'yellow dog cowardice'?"

"What are trying to do?" Hiram said, his sneer returning. "Unnerve me by hurling insults?"

"I know better than that. You've probably been called every lowdown name there is."

"And 'gunslinger' is a title of high stature?"

"I prefer gun *fighter*. It has more class."

Hiram barked a nasty laugh. "What a joke. I haven't seen anyone with even a hint of class since I got this side of the Sierras."

"Careful. You'll insult your latest bunch of hired thugs."

"I pay them enough so they can afford to be insulted and not worry about it."

"That's real interesting." J.D.'s eyes narrowed. "And how much are the Ballard brothers paying you? Enough that you can afford to end up with a bellyful of lead in a six-foot hole in the ground out here on the side of this no-class mountain?"

"They're paying me a hell of a lot more than that ungrateful whore is paying you to risk your neck for her."

J.D. stood with the Winchester gripped in his raised right hand, resting across his shoulder. Close to his ear, he could hear the wood fibers of the stock section above the cocking lever creak quietly as his grip tightened.

"How *is* the slut paying you, anyway? From the money she'll inherit off her fool of a husband? Or are you taking it out in trade? But where would that leave your pretty little wifc? Oh, wait a minute...now I remember. Kinky three-way sessions were always a specialty of Belle's. And I guess it stands to reason that any gal like that blonde of yours, who totes a pistol and makes her way as a gunslinger—excuse me, I mean gun *fighter*—probably is inclined toward wishing she had a *meat pistol,* too, so that would make her—"

"Shut your filthy mouth!" The words exploded out of J.D.

"Before you swing that rifle into play, stop and think!" warned Hiram. "Not about payment, but about cost—the risk of costing you and your wife your lives. And for what? For a lousy goddamn whore?"

Inside the ruins, Kate knew how hard J.D. must be struggling to hold his temper and keep from blasting the foul-mouthed Hiram. She knew, because she was fighting the same battle herself. She had maneuvered into a position where she had a clear shot at Hiram if she'd wanted to take it. But that wasn't the plan...if and when it came to cutting down the piece of slime, then it was J.D.'s call to make.

Besides, should shooting break out, Kate had plenty to occupy her attention right in her immediate surroundings.

She harbored no fantasy that she'd made it this far without being spotted. She, in turn, had spotted one of Hiram's hirelings and had a pretty good idea where another was. In the latter case, it wasn't that she had seen or heard anything specific, but rather a matter of *sensing* there was someone there. Such feelings had proven accurate enough in the past to mean never ignoring one. At any rate, when the fireworks inevitably popped, there wasn't going to be the need to hunt for a target. What it would come down to was who could shoot the fastest and most accurately. In the sooty shadows where she was hunkered down, Kate smiled a thin, confident smile...she liked her chances.

◆◇◆

"If everybody keeps cool heads and plays this smart," J.D. responded to Hiram, "there may be a way to do this without costing *any* more lives."

"I don't think so. But I'm willing to listen."

"It's real easy. You give the right answer to a simple question and then agree to go back to Frisco and never bother Belle again, we call it even and call it quits."

Hiram grunted disdainfully. "What I thought. Nothing but a bucket of hog slop. In the first place, you've got no kind of advantage to be making the call on anything. You're covered by more guns than your stupid cowboy brain can probably count. Same for little wifey. Shame to have to blast a doll like her to pieces. But it looks like we're not going to have a choice because, in the second place, there's no way in hell I'm going back to Frisco without Belle. Dead or alive."

"What sense does that make? She can't earn money dead. Even alive, she'll never earn back what the Ballards have paid you to chase her clear the hell out here."

As if by rote, Hiram said, "It's a matter of principle. And it sends a message to any other whore who might be thinking about trying the same stunt."

The coolness circulating through J.D. suddenly turned ice cold. It was a familiar feeling to him, the one that signaled a situation had reached the point where there was nothing left but to start throwing lead. "Any message sent back to Frisco by you," he said in a tone as chill as the way he felt inside, "is going to have to come from Hell."

In the same instant, J.D. shrugged the Yellowboy off his shoulder and swung it down and forward in a swift, smooth motion. The forestock slapped solidly into the cupped palm of the left hand he reached out to brace the barrel. Simultaneously, his finger stroked the trigger and the first shot roared out. As fast as he could lever rounds into the chamber, J.D. fired twice more, aiming low, meaning to cut Hiram's legs out but leave him alive.

With surprising speed, Hiram yanked the pistol from the sash around his waist and was thrusting it toward J.D. when the first slug hit him in the right thigh, just above the knee. He screamed and twisted away, managing to snap off a wild shot that went harmlessly high and wide. Another of J.D.'s shots chewed into the dirt, but the third one also hit Hiram, shattering his left ankle. Hiram screamed again.

The two men hit the ground at the same time—Hiram because he had no choice, J.D. because he knew he needed to duck away from the volley of shots that were certain to be coming his way. He was right. No sooner had he landed on his stomach and began scrambling for the cover of some brush tangled around the trunk of a young cottonwood than bullets sizzled through the air above his head and went slapping through the scrub growth near where he'd been standing.

◆◇◆

At the sight of J.D. swinging his Winchester into play, even before he triggered his first round, Kate sprang into action. She knew for certain where one of Hiram's concealed gunnies was, and she also knew that *he* knew where she was. So, as her Colt leaped into her fist, she pitched herself hard to the left—lunging four feet away from where the gunny would be aiming—and squeezed off a shot while she was still in mid-air. Exactly as she'd calculated, the gunny was spinning and firing at where she had *been* when her slug caught him high in the chest, just below his Adam's apple, slamming him back and down.

A calculation Kate had failed to make, however, was to take into consideration how much dust and loose soot had accumulated on the skeleton of timbers amidst the hotel ruins. When she landed and rolled—intending to rise up and swing her Colt toward where she had sensed the second gunny was—she bumped against an upright board tilted against some horizontal ones and a boiling, blinding, choking shower of black granules was knocked loose to rain down on her.

She fell back, coughing and cursing, eyes burning. A pair of shots rang out and smacked into blackened timbers uncomfortably close, dislodging more soot. Kate fired blindly in the direction she thought the shots had come from and then ducked down, squirming to find cover under the roiling clouds of smothering blackness.

◆◇◆

Out on the flat in front of the hotel, J.D. was also squirming low to find cover from the lead pouring hot and heavy in his direction. Like he'd anticipated, Hiram had placed two shooters in the trees down by the creek. But the satisfaction of having that anticipation proven out wasn't gaining him much right at the moment, not with the pair of them bent on trying to blow his head off. The one thing he had going for him, though, was that the damn fools were armed only with handguns, diminishing their accuracy at the distance involved. With his Winchester, he was able to make it hot for them in return and, if given just a glimmer of a target, to do so with truer results.

The flip side of that, unfortunately, was the fact he couldn't concentrate solely on the creek shooters because he had Hiram and however many gunmen were inside the hotel ruins—at least until Kate took care of them—to worry about from the other side.

Whimpering and cursing and mewling in pain, Hiram was crawling raggedly across the ground, trying to gain the cover of the tall stone chimney. He still gripped his gun in one hand and, twice now, he had reached behind himself and fired again at J.D., but without really aiming.

"Keep that bastard pinned down, boys!" he hollered as he crawled. "My legs are shot to hell, but don't let him kill me!"

"Stop crawling and lay still! Throw your gun away and call your dogs off, I'll let you live," J.D. offered, still hoping to try and keep Hiram alive long enough to get an answer on whether he had anything to do with the killing of Oliver Braedon.

"You go to hell!" Hiram's voice trembled with pain and rage and fear.

A fresh volley from the tree line shooters forced J.D. to flatten and hug the ground once more.

He wondered what was going on in the ruins. There'd been shooting from inside—though none of it aimed his way, from what he could tell—only then it had gone quiet. He felt a pang of concern for Kate, but was forced to sharply remind himself that she could take care of herself. What was more, he couldn't do her any good if he allowed himself to be distracted and ended up with a bullet through his skull.

J.D. guardedly swung his attention back toward the creek, peering around the cottonwood trunk and through an opening low in the brush. When the six-gun fire eased up momentarily, he was ready. All he needed was—There! He saw a wink of sunlight reflected off a gun barrel and almost before the wink had faded the butt of the Yellowboy bucked against his shoulder, sending a slug sizzling across the flat and into whoever was holding the gun. J.D. heard a shrill yip of pain and then a man's limp body spilled forward out of the foliage to flop and remain motionless on the ground.

J.D. jerked back behind the tree trunk as two rounds of return fire were sent his way. Glancing over at Hiram, who continued to crawl toward the ruins, leaving a trail of stringy blood in the dust, J.D. emitted a taunting laugh and called to him. "Your saviors are falling fast, Hiram. And the one who's left can't shoot for shit!"

Hiram had dragged himself nearly to the chimney. If he gained its cover and still had the strength to do some more shooting, he could become a serious threat. J.D. knew he ought to finish him right then and there, regardless of any unanswered questions. But, damn, the thought of shooting a wounded man in the back of the head while he was crawling away on the ground brought out a gag reflex in J.D. that was almost more than he could choke down.

◆◇◆

Kate was still struggling to regain her vision inside the old hotel. She lay very still, wedged deep in a pile of crumbling debris and a thick layer of sediment that had accumulated over what had once been the floor of the hotel. Her only movement was the minimal wiping motion of her left thumb, trying to clear enough gunk out of her watering eyes to be able to see. In her right hand she now gripped the fully loaded Starr revolver.

The only thing keeping her alive, she judged, was the cloud of soot and dust still hanging in the air around her—obscuring her from the second shooter almost as much as her temporary blindness was making him invisible to her.

But she could hear him moving, edging closer to make sure of his kill. Faint crunching and whispery snatches of noise as he brushed too close to a charred timber reached her ears. The sporadic shooting from out front helped mask the sound of his movement, but at least it also told Kate that J.D. was still in the thick of the fighting.

As she continued to blink and wipe the gummy wetness from her eyes, Kate realized her vision was starting to improve from nothing to being able to vaguely discern blurry shapes and outlines. Her heart hammered and her grip on the Starr tightened. Yes! Now, if only...

And then, almost directly in front of her, one of the blurred shapes *moved*. The second shooter was right there, practically on top of her! Kate's mind raced. The only thing she could think was that she was sunk so deep in debris and sediment and so blackened by all the soot that had gotten dumped on her that, through the further impediment of the haze still hanging in the air, the shooter could not see her. He, on the other hand, standing upright against the light from outside, was easily outlined, even to her limited sight.

But the why and wherefore didn't really matter. What mattered was taking advantage of this turnabout in what only moments ago had seemed a nearly hopeless predicament.

Kate raised the Starr, aiming upward at the shape hovering over her, and emptied four chambers as fast as she could squeeze the trigger. The shape gave a single loud grunt of surprise and then fell back, twisting before toppling all the way down, his spasming trigger finger discharging two rounds off into the bright sunlight that had betrayed him.

◆◇◆

J.D. was relieved to hear the renewed gunfire from within the ruins. It was assurance that Kate was still alive and fighting.

A moment later, however, that same gunfire resulted in quite a different reaction.

Both of the wild, dying shots thrown by the man-shape Kate had blasted came screaming out of the ruins and, totally inadvertently, slammed into the tall chimney that had managed to remain standing for so long after the rest of the hotel was only a pile of refuse...The same chimney behind which Hiram was so desperately trying to reach for cover. The bullets slamming into the weathered, wind-scoured pile of stones did what the elements hadn't yet been able to accomplish. The top half of the tall structure teetered momentarily above the weakened chinks knocked out by the errant slugs and then came crashing ingloriously down.

Down directly on top of Hiram Woolsey.

Chapter 18

It was the following morning before J.D. and Kate rode out of Silver Dog.

Following the violence at the old hotel, it had taken less time to appease the inquiries of the authorities, as represented by a hastily assembled Miners Council, than it had for Kate to scrub herself clean from the grime she ended up covered in.

Hank Brimbel played a helpful hand in each matter.

First, she testified how it had been the man identified as Hiram Woolsey who'd initiated the meeting that resulted in the shootout. In the course of her telling, Hank included the clear impression she'd gotten of Hiram's dangerous intentions. This dovetailed well with the identities of the three additional dead bodies found at the scene. All were known troublemakers with criminal pasts who'd shown up in Silver Dog after the spring thaw, getting by on gambling and hiring out to do grunt work for anyone foolish enough to trust hiring them.

A fourth cohort of theirs seemed to be suddenly missing from the area. It seemed logical to figure he'd been the second shooter down by the creek and had apparently fled after seeing his employer crushed under the collapsing chimney and then realizing his pals were all cut down.

After that much was settled, Hank had invited the Blazes to stay the night at her place. The offer included the chance for Kate to soak as long as she wanted in the oversized bathtub that Hank's late husband, a man of considerable girth, had specially installed back when he was still alive. With that secondary provision, there was never the slightest question of refusing the offer. As a show of appreciation for her hospitality, Kate and J.D. took Hank out to Stroheim's that evening for supper.

♦◊♦

Despite everybody else—including even Kate, to a certain extent—seemingly willing to accept that Hiram must have had a hand in killing Oliver Braedon, J.D. remained stubbornly doubtful. It was for this reason that he continued to be troubled as he and Kate rode back into Elk City. He was, of course, pleased that they'd caught up with Hiram in order to hold him to account for the things he *had* done and to remove him as a threat to Belle; but he nevertheless regretted failing to keep him alive long enough to answer the question concerning Oliver.

As it turned out, however, in one of those bizarrely unexpected twist of events, the answer was awaiting them when they arrived at the Big Thompson Lodge. Almost as surprising as the revelation was the contingent gathered to deliver it.

As soon as they got to the lodge, after stabling their horses but before going to their own quarters, J.D. and Kate stopped by Belle's suite to update her on how it had gone with Hiram and to check on the condition of Sam Ruckner. The first big surprise came in the form of the four Braedon offspring who were present in the suite as the Blazes were ushered in. From the somber expressions worn by everyone, J.D. immediately presumed the group was on hand to cause more trouble.

The first order of business was still to determine that

Sam—who was out in the parlor with the others, propped up on pillows in a large easy chair—was doing well, and then to report their successful trackdown of Hiram. With the presence of so many others, they couldn't go into too many details for fear of revealing the ambusher's link to Belle's past.

With that much out of the way, it was time to face whatever purpose the Braedons were there for. What was then related to the Blazes was a stunning occurrence that had taken place in that very room earlier in the day.

It all stemmed from a visit by Maria Sandimez, the cook and housekeeper who had served the Braedons for so many years. She'd shown up asking for a word with Belle. Once inside, she immediately pulled a Colt's Dragoon pistol from under her shawl and proceeded to unleash a furious verbal attack on Belle while all the time menacing her with the heavy caliber gun.

As she talked, Maria spoke of the passion and deep feelings that had blossomed between her and Oliver Braedon and the secret affair they'd carried on during the later years of the first Mrs. Braedon's illness, and then beyond. In Maria's mind, *she* was to have been the next Mrs. Braedon and her boy Jorge would have been raised as another of Oliver's sons.

But then Oliver had met Belle and brought her home as his new wife. Maria was crushed, to the point of considering suicide in her pain and shame. When she told this to Oliver, he talked her out of it. He told her that he would always have deep feelings for her and that he would always take care of her and Jorge, that they were part of the family. For Jorge's sake, she relented and continued on, hiding her inner torment. She found consolation from simply being *near* Oliver, convincing herself that his infatuation with the much younger and obviously superficial Belle would wear thin and he would come to his senses. At that point he would also remember the depth of his true love for Maria, would come crawling back to her, and then they would be together the way it was meant to be.

Instead, the day came when realization finally hit Maria how pathetic and hopeless her groveling fantasies really were. It was the day Oliver and Belle came back from looking at the property where they were going to build their new house (the same day they were re-accosted by Hiram and then encountered the Blazes, though none of that was ever spoken of). Maria overheard them talking upon their return and it struck her like a thunderbolt that once Oliver and Belle moved away and Clay and his healthy young wife moved into the big house, there would be no need—no place—for her and Jorge. Everything Oliver had told her was a lie! From the furtive lust she had mistaken for love all those years ago, while his wife lay dying in another room, clear on through to his false promises to always take care of her and her son.

Maria seethed. This time she did not contemplate taking her own life. No, this time she instead felt a determination to take the life of the man who had abused and shamed and lied to her.

Later that afternoon, when Oliver went out to check on Jorge in the carriage shed, the rage inside Maria had built to an explosive level. She took the Henry rifle down from over the kitchen door that lead outside—kept there to use on coyotes or other varmints who showed up in the back yard, a weapon Oliver himself had taught Maria how to shoot—and carried it out behind the corral fence in the lengthening shadows cast by the approach of evening.

When Oliver came walking back toward the house, she pumped two slugs into him.

◆◇◆

"From the sound of it," said Clay Braedon, who, along with Belle, had been relating the story up to this point, "she probably was intending to go back in the house and shoot Belle, too. But the quick flurry of activity in response to those first two shots apparently caused her to change her mind."

"So she waited," said Belle. "She waited, but she never stopped seething and hating. This morning, for whatever reason, she must have figured she'd waited long enough. She had Jorge drive her into town, sent him on some errands, then came here to complete her business with me."

For the first time, Sam Ruckner spoke. His head was hung low, he didn't lift his face to make eye contact with anyone. "I was in the other room, in my sick bed. I heard the voices out here, recognized that one of 'em belonged to Maria. In all the years, I'd never heard her talk so loud or in such an angry tone. So I crawled out of bed and came to see what was wrong. For some reason, I'll never quite understand why, I took time to hook my six-gun out of its holster hanging off the back of a chair..."

Sam paused for a long minute. He still didn't raise his head. J.D. could hear him swallow. When he started talking again, there was a quaver to the first few words. "When I opened the door, I right away saw Maria standing there, poking that big Dragoon at Mrs. Braedon. At first I didn't know what in tarnation was going on, but...but the things Maria was saying made it clear quick enough. When she turned her head to see me standing there, the look on her face changed...I'll never forget how her expression turned...sad, it seemed, and hurt. Like she was sorry for me to see her like she was...But then it went right back to being all angry again. Her eyes swung once more to Mrs.

Braedon and she raised the Dragoon a little higher. I could see her knuckles start to turn white as her grip tightened and...I had no choice but to stop her. I only meant to shoot her in the arm or shoulder, but when I jerked up my six-gun I bumped my hand on the edge of the door frame and it threw my aim off...I...I..."

"We know the rest, Sam," Belle said gently. "You don't have to go through it again."

Sam's shoulders trembled with silent sobs. His torment was obvious, but J.D. suspected he might be the only one looking on who understood the full extent of the man's torment for killing the woman he'd loved from afar for so many years.

"What about the boy? Jorge?" Kate asked quietly.

"He's devastated, to be sure," answered Nora Braedon. "We sent for some of the wranglers from our ranch and they're with him now. We'll make sure he's not alone in the days ahead."

"Next to Maria and Pa," added Curtis, the youngest brother, "I was about as close to Jorge as anybody. I'll see that he gets looked after."

Sam spoke again, finally lifting his head. "There was a time when I was pretty close to the youngster, too. Hell, I was there the night he was born." He cut his moist eyes to Curtis. "You do that, lad. You make sure to look after Jorge."

"What about you, Sam?" said Belle. "You'll still be around."

Sam shook his head. "No. No, I won't...Soon as I'm fit enough to travel, it'll be time and past time for me to move on."

"You don't have to do that, you know," Clay told him. "Not because of anything that was said before...not by either side. That was tempers talking, but the foolishness of

132

that kind of thing is painfully evident now and we need to get past it and learn from it.

"Speaking for my brothers and our sister, we've come to realize that if we'd been focused less on our petty greed and unfounded suspicions and had paid closer attention to what was going on practically under our noses...well, a number of things might have turned out different." Clay sighed raggedly. "We've already expressed all of this to Belle and we're calling off our lawyer as far as how to work things out, just within the family...But that still leaves you, Sam. Any time you want, you're welcome back at the Bar OB."

"That goes for me, too. Double for me," Chuck Braedon was quick to say. "In your case, it was my temper and my mouth barking the loudest. I'm real sorry, Sam. Like Clay said, you belong back at the ranch."

Sam smiled wistfully. "Obliged for the kind words, boys. From both of you. I'm glad you kids are showing signs of having your heads screwed on straight after all. And I got no hard feelings...This valley will always hold good memories for me. But now, it also holds some mighty bad ones. I 'spect I'll bounce back from this bullet hole quick enough. But it's gonna take some distance and considerable time before I ever heal from...well, you understand."

Nobody said anything for a minute. Then, her words coming in something of a rush, Belle broke the silence. "Speaking of that bullet wound, you're beginning to look exhausted. I think it's time to get you back to your bed. The doctor will be stopping by in a bit and if he sees I've let you overdo it, he'll chew me out royally."

Sam mumbled a token protest, but it was easy to see that he was weary enough to actually welcome the inevitable. Especially when Kate and Nora closed in to give Belle a hand in getting him up and into the other room.

As the three ladies escorted the wounded man away,

Chuck Braedon stepped over to J.D. "Sayin' sorry to Sam was only part of what I owe." He extended his right hand. "I wouldn't blame you if you slapped it away. But I hope you won't. I hope you'll accept my apologies to you as well...along with my thanks."

J.D. shook the offered hand. Frowning, he said, "'Thanks'?"

Grinning crookedly, Chuck said, "For not blowin' my stupid head off either of those times I tried to goad you into a gun fight."

Epilogue

Later that night, J.D. and Kate lay together in the spacious, cushiony bed of their suite.

"Do you realize," murmured Kate, "how little time we've actually spent relaxing on this so-called vacation of ours?"

"Isn't that what we're doing now?" J.D. responded sleepily.

"Finally, yes."

"Okay. So we'll extend our stay a little longer."

"But, even with everything relatively settled, do you think we'd really be left alone, left strictly to our own pursuits if we lingered here?"

"We would if we drew a hard line. Made it damn clear that's the way we wanted it."

"Maybe." But Kate didn't sound very convinced. "I think we'd have a far better chance, though, if we took another crack at this vacation thing in another location."

"You got some place particular in mind?" J.D. asked, already suspecting that she did.

"Well, we've still got a pretty fair amount of money saved ahead...I've often wondered about San Francisco. I know you've been there, but I never have. For years I've heard people rave about it—the City by the Bay, the Golden Gate, Chinatown, and on and on." J.D. could feel her shoulders move in a faint shrug under the covers next to him. "I always knew I wanted to visit there some day, I'm just thinking that now might be a good time, that's all."

WAYNE D. DUNDEE

J.D. lifted himself on one elbow. "And, in addition to all those things you just rattled off, did you happen to recall that San Fran is also home to the Ballard brothers—Belle's former employers, and the fine gentlemen responsible for sending Hiram after her?"

"Well. Now that you mention it..."

"Are you serious?"

Now Kate raised on her elbow, too. "Yes, J.D., I'm dead serious. Do you think for a minute those two maniacs are just going to give up, especially once they get the news Hiram has been eliminated? If they were so hell bent before to go to all the trouble they did to reclaim or kill Belle as an example to dissuade others, what makes anyone think they wouldn't add revenge to their list of reasons and be even more fiercely determined to send somebody else after her?"

J.D. didn't respond right away. Then: "You've really become a champion for Belle, haven't you?"

"She deserves a break, J.D. She got one when she met and married Oliver, but it didn't last very long. She came so far, came so close. Then Oliver got killed and his children turned against her and she almost had it all yanked away. Not to boast, but if not for us, for what we were able to do, it very likely would have come to that."

"But we *were* here, and were able to help it turn out better. Not perfect, not considering the lives that were lost and others shattered. But I think Clay and his siblings are sincere about working things out with Belle. If she makes the choice to stick around, she can still have a pretty decent life in this valley."

"Not if the Ballards send somebody else after her. Somebody perhaps even worse than Hiram. In addition to the physical threat, she'd be facing the risk all over again of her past being revealed. How long do you think Clay and the others would remain so accommodating if that came out?"

136

J.D. expelled a long, slow breath. "So the only way to be sure—to finish what we started when we decided to get involved in this to begin with—is to go to San Francisco and deal directly with the Ballards."

"As it is, like you pointed out a minute ago," Kate said quietly, "lives have been lost and others shattered. Did we go through that only to leave an opening for more of the same?"

Again J.D. didn't say anything right away. When he did, he said, "I've got one more question."

"And that is?"

"When we get to Frisco, will you want to enjoy the sights and sounds of the city first...or wait until *after* we've taken care of the Ballards?"

J.D. and Kate Blaze are two of the deadliest gunfighters the Old West has ever seen. They also happen to be husband and wife, as passionate in their love for each other as they are in their quest for justice on the violent frontier!

BLAZE! is the first novel in a thrill-packed, all-new Adult Western series created by bestselling action/adventure author Stephen Mertz. J.D. and Kate find themselves facing a deadly ambush by Apaches, then they're hired to track down a gang of ruthless outlaws led by the beautiful, savage bandit queen Rosa Diablo. It's gun-swift excitement all the way in this gritty tale from Stephen Mertz.

Future novels in this series will be written by some of the top storytellers in the business, including Robert J. Randisi, legendary creator of The Gunsmith and author of more than 600 novels, and the award-winning and critically acclaimed Wayne D. Dundee. Rough Edges Press is proud to present...*BLAZE!*

Husband and wife gunfighters Kate and J.D. Blaze are hired to track down a gang of rustlers, but what they don't know is that they're going to find themselves in the middle of a three-cornered war, playing each side against the others. If they're lucky they'll collect three payoffs instead of one...but will those payoffs be in gold—or hot lead?!

Legendary Western author Robert J. Randisi, creator of The Gunsmith, joins the *Blaze!* team with this fast-action novel of treachery, revenge, passion, and blistering gunplay. From the finest hotels in Denver to a savage showdown in a ghost town, *The Deadly Guns* is adventure all the way!

Made in United States
North Haven, CT
21 July 2022

21624531R00078